ANGEL BLUE

A Spy High novel

By A. J. Butcher

Spy High Series One
1. The Frankenstein Factory
2. The Chaos Connection
3. The Serpent Scenario
4. The Paranoia Plot
5. The Soul Stealer
6. The Annihilation Agenda

Spy High Series Two
Edward Red
Angel Blue
Benjamin White
Calista Green
Jake Black
Agent Orange

ANGEL BLUE

A Spy High novel

A. J. Butcher

www.atombooks.co.uk

A paperback original from *Atom* Books

First published in Great Britain by Atom 2004

Based on concepts devised by Ben Sharpe
Story by A. J. Butcher

A CIP catalogue record for this book is available from the British Library.

ISBN 1 90423 335 X

Typeset in Cochin by M Rules
Printed and bound in Great Britain
by Bookmarque Ltd, Croydon

Atom
An imprint of
Time Warner Book Group UK
Brettenham House
Lancaster Place
London WC2E 7EN

www.twbg.co.uk

For Rodd and Jill
Blue was always the colour

PROLOGUE

Night again, and if she had any sense she'd be some-where else. Walking barefoot on the beach with the boy of her dreams, maybe, or making out under cover of darkness like any normal seventeen year old girl. But no. Instead, Lori Angel was scaling the perimeter wall of a drug baron's estate in the heart of Bolivia, camouflaged, sleepshot wristbands securely in place and shock blaster present and correct in its shoulder holster. Being a graduate of Spy High was cool for sure, but it played hell with your social life.

At the top of the wall she crouched, lithe like a cat poised to spring. Lorenzo hadn't bothered to stud the concrete with broken glass or decorate it with barbed wire. He was obviously of the opinion that the cameras stationed along the wall at ten metre intervals and swiv-elling like aliens' eyeballs were more than adequate to detect and deter any rash trespassers. He was probably right, too, for intruders *not* garbed in a Spy High issue chameleon suit. Unfortunately for him, Lori was model-ling the top of the range.

It was clear, however, that the suit had been designed by someone with a background in infiltration and espionage techniques rather than fashion. It came in one colour only, what her old team-mate Eddie had christened secret agent black, and while it clung to the body like skin, the single-piece garment was unflattering in every other respect, particularly the hood, which covered the head entirely and lacked even holes for eyes or a slit for a mouth. It wasn't the kind of gear Lori would choose to go clubbing in but when penetrating the headquarters of the average madman, megalomaniac or would-be ruler of the world, it was the first thing she reached for in the wardrobe.

Lori dropped nimbly to earth. The best the cameras might have done was to identify a slight flickering in the air as she moved. Because once activated, the millions of nano-chips woven into the chameleon suit's fabric instantly assimilated and then replicated the physical details of the immediate environment; they also masked the wearer's breathing, heat signature and other tell-tale signs of existence. Effectively, a chameleon suit rendered you invisible.

So Lori could afford to pause and survey the grounds ahead of her through the hood's infra-red viewing panels. Not that she loitered for long. One thing the suit couldn't do was complete her mission for her.

Besides, she was worried about Jake.

Senses alert, she loped through the trees. The lights of Lorenzo's fortress of a house were still far ahead. There was the energy barrier to negotiate first, then the guards. No, Lori corrected herself, there should be no such word as *then* in an agent's vocabulary, not while on active duty. There should only be *now*. And the now was the barrier.

Here it was in front of her, superficially as invisible to her eye as she was to it, but she'd have known it was there even without the briefing. The arc of suspiciously cleared foliage extending to her right and left, interrupted only by the stalks of plants that refused to sway in the night breeze like their companions, chiefly because they weren't organic at all but metal and wire, were a pretty big giveaway.

Lori stepped towards the energy barrier. No doubt it contained serious electricity, enough current to fry her until her skin was as charcoal-black as her suit, until she could have attended a fancy dress party as Joan of Arc *after* her little rendezvous with the stake and impressed everyone with the authenticity of her costume. But the chameleon suit was already living up to its name. Its nano-chips fed new information into its circuits, adapted to the notion of a barrier, the nature of its energy. The marginal increase in its wearer's output of perspiration the suit also compensated for without complaint.

Lori passed through the barrier unscathed.

And then she was running again, with only human barriers between her and Lorenzo now – between she and Jake and the beginning of the end of the drug lord's entire Rush operation.

Rush. The boy's face was still in her mind, like a scene from a movie you wish you'd never seen but which you can't make yourself forget. The drug was like a time machine that had transported him decades closer to his death. It had ravaged his flesh and blinded his eyes and made claws of his hands and he'd been shuddering and shaking and convulsing. Convulsing uncontrollably, convulsing for ever. And his lips, a grey colour like the ashes of a fire or the remains of cigarettes, they'd tried to form words. From their random shivers and twitches, they'd tried to say something. Lori had thought it was 'help me', or maybe she'd *liked* to think so.

There'd been other boys too, no shortage of victims of Rush to be introduced to. And girls, lots of girls, bent into crones by their addiction. Jake had been affected most by the girls. He'd be thinking of them now, Lori knew.

Which was why she had no time to waste.

The outer grounds gave way to formal gardens, to statuary in marble and jade. Ancient Rome transported to the New World courtesy of drug money and human misery. The moon was full, but Lori could have found her way in pitch blackness – she and Jake had practised the mission in virtual reality so many times. The pools came next, linked together like an irrigation system rather than a leisure facility. Ahead, near enough now to distinguish its individual windows and the crenellations on its castle roof without the aid of telescopic vision, were the six storeys of Mickey Lorenzo's house. Mickey Lorenzo himself inside. According to their briefing, he liked to spend his evenings composing sonatas on the baby grand in his bedroom.

Lori scanned the sheer wall she was approaching. But Lorenzo's bedroom had no window, no point of egress to the outside world at all. To foil sniper fire. Apparently, Mickey Lorenzo harboured a fear of assassination. Hence the wall and the cameras. Hence the energy barrier.

Hence the guards.

They patrolled the grounds close to the house in pairs, like lovers or London buses. Lori knew their routes and their habits better than they did themselves. She knew how much time she had to work in.

She was waiting for them when they rounded the corner, sullen and bearded and looking right through her. She could have eliminated them with her eyes closed, if to do so had not been unprofessional. The second man had barely the chance to register the sudden, sighing collapse of his partner before he too was struck square in the chest by a sleepshot shell. Immediate unconsciousness guaranteed.

Applause. A dark chuckle from thin air.

Lori was too well trained to start. It could only be Jake. It was, his lean form developing beside her like a living photograph as he deactivated his chameleon suit. 'Was beginning to think you weren't coming,' he whispered, unperturbed that he seemed to be addressing an empty space. 'Was about to take these two out myself. What kept you?'

'Nothing *kept* me, Jake.' Lori pressed the stud on her belt that admitted her own presence. 'I'm on time. You're early.'

'Better than being late.' He pulled back his hood, revealing tangled hair as dark as nightfall. There was a wild spark in his eyes, and the strongly defined features that Lori knew so well – with their brooding, somehow dangerous appeal – were twisted now into what seemed to Lori to be becoming an habitual scowl. 'What's Deveraux's obsession with timetables, anyway? As long as we get the job done that's all that matters.'

Lori decided not to argue the point. She simply removed her own hood. Their arrest of Mickey Lorenzo was to be undertaken as a team, and in teamwork it always helped to be able to see your partner. The chameleon suits had served their purpose. She shook long blonde hair free and fixed steely blue eyes on Jake. 'So what are we waiting for? Let's get the guards out of the way.'

They dragged the fallen men's bodies into the concealing shadows of the grove that fringed the path. Lori checked the watch set into her sleepshot wristband. 'Good. We still have a minute before the next patrol's scheduled to pass this side of the house.'

'Who cares? Let 'em come,' Jake hissed recklessly. 'It won't be *us* regretting it. Let 'em come.'

'Jake,' cautioned Lori. 'We have to keep to the plan, at least until something goes wrong.'

'Something *always* goes wrong,' Jake retorted cynically. 'Why don't we just expect the worst and improvise *now*? Sometimes you sound a lot like Ben, Lori.'

Lori couldn't keep the hurt from her expression at that. No, Jake, she wanted to correct him, sometimes it still seems as if you're a raw, inexperienced student spy at the Deveraux College rather than a seasoned, mission-hardened graduate agent who should have learned long ago that following the rules is the safest and surest way to stay alive. And sometimes, she wanted to say, sometimes, Jake, when you throw my old relationship with Ben in my face like that, like a challenge, sometimes I find it hard to believe that we've been more than just good friends for over a year now. Or that in another year we'll still be together.

But what Lori actually said was, 'Are you finished?'

Jake frowned at himself, suddenly abashed. 'Yeah, I'm finished. I guess. Sorry, Lori, it's just, thinking about Lorenzo and Rush and what that filth does to you, I just . . .' He formed helpless fists. 'It's not good.'

'I know,' Lori said, laying her hands over his consolingly. 'And we're going to put an end to it.' She lifted her eyes to the house. 'Thirty seconds to make the window.'

'With clingskin?' The scowl became a grin. Which was better. 'That's not even a race.'

The gloves and boots of their suits impregnated with Spy High's miracle adhesive, Lori and Jake spidered up the side of the house as effortlessly as they'd climbed the perimeter wall. They knew exactly where they were going, which window would provide access to the third floor landing and from there to Mickey Lorenzo's private rooms. The window was closed but that was no problem. Every Spy High agent's belt contained a tiny glass-cutter for just such an eventuality. Lori wielded hers with a surgeon's skill, though few medical procedures were carried out while glued precariously halfway up a building.

'If Eddie was here,' noted Jake, thinking suddenly of their wise-cracking former team-mate, 'he'd be saying he was stuck on you or something lame like that, don't you reckon, Lo?'

Lori sliced open the window. 'Probably. And what about you, Jake?'

'What about me?'

'Are you still stuck on me, too?' She didn't look at him, confined her gaze to the smaller square she'd cut within the shape of the window.

'Of course I am,' he reacted, perhaps a little defensively. 'What kind of question is that?'

'I don't know. A paranoid one.' Lori used the suction of her clingskinned fingers to pull the severed glass free of the window-frame. Jake took hold of it with one hand. She looked at him now. 'I'm glad.' And was snaking inside the house before her partner could respond.

Drawing her shock blaster. Absorbing her surroundings in the split-second permissible. It was just as the briefing had promised: a broad landing, lushly carpeted, sweeping round to a central staircase that descended to the ground floor like a marble waterfall. The architecture was ornate, overstated, the sign of a vain and self-important man. Statues of the classical gods sentried along the landing, down the stairs, but they were deities all adorned with the same face. The bulging brow, the thick lips, the crooked nose broken in a brawl when he was young – Mickey Lorenzo.

From a further distance along the landing, a piano playing.

Three guards were in the ground floor reception area below, grouped together and talking relaxedly, not thinking to glance up, not suspecting that they were already well on the way to failing in their duty to protect their employer. So far, so according to plan.

Lori took the sheet of window from Jake, propped it silently against the wall while he swung himself inside to join her. She pointed in the direction of the music. He nodded.

Lori noted that the scowl was coming back.

Still, if the mission continued in the text-book style it had established so far, that wouldn't matter. If they could just steal their way into Lorenzo's rooms without interruption, subdue him without injury, smuggle him to the roof, then signal . . .

She'd almost forgotten again. No thens. Only nows.

As in, now a door was opening immediately ahead of them and someone was staggering out on to the landing. Someone laughing, but emptily, like an echo in an asylum. Someone the Deveraux agents both recognised from their briefing. Someone they knew would be in the building, but who was not in the plan.

Stephanie Lorenzo, the drug dealer's fifteen-year-old daughter.

She was dressed in a silk kimono.

It might have been thought that, chancing upon a pair of intruders in your own home clad in black and pointing shock blasters at you would be an encouragement to scream. Instead she saw Lori and Jake and her hands jerked into applause and her laughter grew more shrill and she seemed barely able to stand up. Her eyes rolled in her head like green and white marbles. Her whole body quaking.

Jake knew what it signified. 'She's on Rush,' he breathed in disbelief. 'Lorenzo's got his own daughter hooked on Rush.'

'Party!' the girl cried. 'It's party time!' She reeled towards the banister. 'Party time!' Almost toppled *over* the banister.

The guards below didn't like that. It wouldn't do their careers a lot of good to have been on duty the night Lorenzo's daughter plunged to her death – they'd probably end up joining her. So with shouts of caution and concern, they darted to the staircase.

And that alone might not have jeopardised the mission. If the Deveraux agents had shrunk back, slipped into one of the many rooms, as Lori by instinct was already beginning to do, the situation might have been retrieved. It was doubtful the guards would believe anything a drugged-up Stephanie might say. But Jake was not retreating into the shadows, he was lunging forward. Like Lorenzo's men, though for more selfless reasons, he didn't want the girl to fall. He grabbed her arm, yanked her away from danger.

Was seen.

The guards sprouted guns as if by magic. They yelled for the alarm to be raised.

The damage was done.

And maybe, Lori thought later, the turning point had really come moments earlier, when Jake first realised that Stephanie Lorenzo was on Rush. That was when the scowl returned to Jake's face – a different kind of addiction.

Nothing for it now, though. Lori opened fire with her sleepshot and the first of Lorenzo's men didn't even make the stairs. Neither did the second. With the third she made it a clean sweep.

The reinforcements, however, announced with the fire of automatic weapons, opted to take cover rather than mount a frontal assault. They'd be more difficult to eliminate.

'Hold them off, Lori,' Jake snapped.

'What?'

'You can do it. I'm going for Lorenzo.' His eyes were cold. 'He's not getting away while we waste our time on these goons.'

'But what about Stephanie?' The girl was writhing in Jake's grasp, shrieking with laughter. 'She could get hit.'

'Good point.' Jake swung the girl around so that she stumbled and sprawled on to the floor. 'Here's the answer. You'll thank me for this when you wake up.' He shot her, once, with sleepshot. Party over. 'Okay, Lori? Follow me when you can.'

'Follow you when I *can*?' Lori watched her partner surge towards Lorenzo's rooms and couldn't help feeling resentment. Jake shouldn't be making unilateral decisions like that, not even in the heat of battle, with bullets riddling the banister and chipping away at the statue of the divine Lorenzo behind which she was sheltering. If anyone should be determining their next move it should be her. It was *Lori* who'd been a team-leader during their student days, not Jake. And with the resentment there was fear, fear of what Jake might do to Mickey Lorenzo when he finally had the drug baron in his sights.

She had to be there with him. She had to act as a calming influence.

And that meant she had to finish off Lorenzo's guards quickly.

Her aim was more accurate than theirs. Sleepshot gradually whittled their numbers down as the more ambitious among them dared forays at the stairs or flashed across the floor to find a better opening, and she still had her shock blaster in reserve. She could probably wreck Lorenzo's reception area in minutes if she switched that to Materials, but with the risk of fatalities if she started simply blowing the place up, to do so was very much a last resort. Life was precious, they'd been taught at Deveraux, even a drug baron's life.

She needed another way to end this fight quickly.

Lori crouched behind the statue, felt in her belt for the gas pellet. Effective over small, enclosed areas only, but guaranteed to induce unconsciousness for three hours. Perfect. She slotted the pellet into the barrel of her shock blaster. The face and arm of the statue came away and shattered on the floor as the guards found their range. From classical to modern art in one burst of gunfire. Lori hunched lower as she flipped the blaster's control to Projectiles.

Sniffing victory, some of Lorenzo's men again tried for the stairs. They'd be sniffing something else soon enough.

Lori rolled from her hiding place, keeping as close to the floor as possible. She fired the blaster from the very top of the staircase. Her assailants scattered, but it did them no good. The pellet exploded in the centre of the reception area, gas instantly billowing in all directions. Lori heard the men coughing as it entered their lungs, saw them floundering as if surprised by a sudden fog. Several managed to escape its influence and reached the higher stairs. Lori couldn't let them miss out on a few hours' shut-eye. Sleepshot resumed its normal service. There was one final stuttering and misguided burst of fire from the guards and then all was still. Or at least, still *enough*. And she couldn't risk leaving Jake alone with Lorenzo any longer.

He'd had the look of somebody ready to kill.

She burst into Mickey Lorenzo's private suite of rooms and at any other time the drug lord might have punished such a liberty with death. Right now, though, he was grovelling on his knees with his hands clasped in abject prayer and begging for life. Jake did not appear to be listening. His finger seemed to be itching to squeeze the trigger of the blaster he had indenting a target on Lorenzo's sweating forehead.

'Jake, don't!'

'Don't what, Lori?' Jake's voice was bitter with anger and disgust. 'Don't put this piece of slime out of his misery? Don't make the world a better place by removing Mickey Lorenzo from it? Don't allow his victims their revenge?'

'Don't do something you'll regret for the rest of your life.' Jake was unmoving, unfeeling. Lori edged closer to Lorenzo, into her partner's line of vision. She'd persuade him with her eyes. Jake had a thing about her eyes.

'The old guilt trip number, huh, Lori?' He sounded dismissive. 'It used to work. But it won't work now. Not any more. Because the Bad Guys, they keep coming back, don't they? And they're always the same. Different faces, yeah, fair enough. And different names. But none of that surface stuff really matters. Inside they're all the same. Inside they're rotten, and the only way to deal with cancer is to cut it out.'

'No, no, please, I implore you, let me live!' Lorenzo groped shamelessly at Jake's boots but the teenager kicked his hands away. 'I'll give you anything, anything. I have money, lots of money. You can have it all. Just don't kill me, please!'

'I wish my Babel chip wasn't working and I didn't understand a word this low-life was saying,' Jake scowled. 'Shut up, you hear me? Shut up!'

Lorenzo whimpered.

'You're not thinking, Jake,' Lori attempted again. 'If we kill Lorenzo . . .'

Jake snorted derisively. 'Don't tell me. I know this one, too. If we kill Lorenzo we bring ourselves down to his level, isn't that how it goes, Lori? We become just as bad as he is, right?'

'Right. Right,' nodded Lorenzo, whose English was obviously better than Jake's Spanish.

Jake's scowl somehow deepened. 'Wrong. That's no argument. That's no sense. So I pull this trigger once. How does that make me as bad as a guy who's sold drugs and supplied drugs to countless people, destroyed thousands of lives? Kids whose futures he's made a fat fortune out of ruining. You saw it, Lori – he's even got his own daughter on the stuff. How can anything *I* do ever be as foul as *that*?'

'You said it yourself, Jake,' Lori pointed out calmly. 'Different crimes. Different wrongs. But only on the surface. Inside they're the same.'

His eyes flickered to hers, and there was a doubt in the dark fire of them, and in that doubt Lori recognised the Jake she knew.

'You know what he was doing when I found him?' Jake nodded towards the grand piano on the other side of the room. 'He was still playing that. Tinkling the ivories while kids die in alleyways with a syringe in their arm. This guy is scum, Lori. I know it and you know it, and he needs to be held to account.'

Lorenzo shrieked as Jake prepared to fire. Lori cried out: 'No!'

But nothing stopped him.

The piano erupted in a discord of snapping wires and blazing keys.

'But I guess . . . there's something in what you say,'

Jake conceded sullenly, and more as a personal favour than in heartfelt conviction. 'I'll give the law another chance. For now.'

For now didn't last long.

They were still at the Deveraux College when the news came through. Supposedly enjoying several days' rest and relaxation before returning to their individual placements and the routine lives of their cover identities. Any possibility of pleasure was lost, however, as soon as they heard.

Lori was only grateful she hadn't actually been with Jake at the time. It gave her an opportunity to steel herself for what was likely to be a volatile conversation.

She wasn't wrong.

'Lori! Hey, Lori!' He caught up with her in one of the corridors in the underground section of the school, Spy High proper, where teenagers were turned into secret agents to battle the villains of tomorrow. 'Where do you think you're going? Trying to avoid me, is it? Well, too bad. We need to talk.'

'Maybe we do,' Lori said, 'but that doesn't mean we need to shout at each other so everyone in the college can hear us. Let's go in here.' She indicated an empty class-room. The present students at Deveraux were between lessons. 'And what are you on about, Jake – trying to avoid you? Why would I want to do that?'

'You've heard, then, haven't you?' Jake deduced craftily. Lori had to admit that she had. Jake repeated the news feed anyway: 'While being transported from the prison to the courthouse, notorious drug baron Miguel 'Mickey' Lorenzo was freed from custody and his guards killed by an unknown number of men assumed to be members of his narcotics operation. Lorenzo's present whereabouts are also unknown, though one of the largest man-hunts blah blah in the history of the world etc and all the little judges and bleeding hearts and the people who make the rules are all no doubt shaking their heads and wringing their hands and asking themselves how could this happen? How could a monster like Lorenzo be on the loose again? You want to offer your services and answer that one, Lori Angel?'

'Lorenzo escaped,' Lori accepted. 'That's bad, I know.' She didn't like the way that Jake was kind of *prowling* up and down, like an animal in a cage that would be deadly if the bars were removed.

'*Bad?* Lorenzo escaped because *we* – you and me, Lori – we put him in a position where he *could* escape. Because *we* delivered him to the authorities healthy and alive and breathing a sigh of relief. Because *you*, Lori, *you* prevented me from doing what needed to be done.'

'Jake, that's not fair – on either of us. We did the right thing. Sparing Lorenzo was the right thing.'

'Oh, great. Cool. The *right thing*.' Jake's sarcasm was venomous. 'That'll make me feel a lot better, that will, when the figures come up on how many new Rush addicts there are on the streets, how many Rush-related deaths thanks to Mickey Lorenzo being back at work. I'll be able to sit back in my chair and put my hands behind my head and smile one of those easy, self-satisfied smiles and say to myself, well, that's nothing to do with me, none of it's my fault. I did the *right thing*.' Jake glowered. 'If what we did was right, Lori, I'd hate to have a wrong thing on my conscience.'

'Jake, you mustn't torture yourself like this. You can't change anything. The authorities'll catch Lorenzo again anyway, you'll see.'

'You want to put money on it? The authorities couldn't catch a cold if they were left naked in the snow. Why do you think they need us? What do you think Spy High is for, Lori? The police and the agencies and the security services are all tied up with so much red tape and bound by so many petty rules and regulations these days that they can't even act any more. We have to defend the people for them. But you know what? When we virtually end up giving guys like Lorenzo a pat on the back and a second chance to go on pushing drugs, I start to wonder what we're all about. Secret agents? Of Toy Town, maybe.'

Lori didn't like to see him this way, bitter, vengeful, *twisted*. 'Jake, listen to me . . .' She reached out to touch him.

He flinched away from her like she was suddenly repellent. 'Keep away from me.'

'Jake?'

'I don't think . . . I don't think there's any point any more.'

'What?' She felt her heart sinking but also, and perhaps more bleakly, a sense of inevitability. 'In *us*? Is that what you mean?'

'That's what I mean. There's no point any more in us . . . being together. I mean, we're not together, are we? Not now, even if we were once. This mission with Lorenzo, it's shown me something, something I can't get over . . .'

'Jake, I thought we could get over anything if we just . . .'

'If we just do what you want, Lori. That's what *you* mean. 'Cause you know what's best, don't you? I'm only an ignorant farmer who scarcely went to school and you're wealthy, well-educated, sophisticated – from the establishment. I need to be told what's right by people like you, people like Ben . . .'

'Oh, we're back to me and Ben now, are we?' Lori sighed with exasperation. 'Jake, haven't you been listening for the past twelve months? Ben is *not* an issue. Ben is not coming between us. I split up with Ben to be with you.'

'Yeah? Well maybe you made the wrong choice, Lori. Like you did with Lorenzo.'

'Are you seriously saying we're over? Just like that?' She was baffled now more than anything else.

'You need to have things in common. For a relationship to work, that's what you need. I mean, more than just the physical stuff . . .'

'But we *have —*'

'We haven't, Lori. Didn't Lorenzo prove that? You're happy with the way things are – playing chase with killers and madmen like the whole thing's a game. Playing by the rules when the rules are stacked in the bad guys' favour. You're content with that. I'm not. I want new rules.' Jake shook his head finally. 'We're done. I'll see you around, Lori.'

And then he was turning to go. Out of the door. Out of her life. She felt compelled to make a last, futile gesture, 'Jake . . .'

And he paused, looked back. 'Take care of yourself.' But it was only a pause.

She was alone. Lori slumped into a chair to register

the fact. Alone again. She'd broken up with Ben for Jake's sake and now Jake had broken up with her. What goes around comes around. And Ben had someone now while she, Lori, had nobody.

And while she sat alone, Lori continued to fail to notice a tiny camera lurking in the corner of the classroom, or to see that it was filming, or to be aware that it *had* been filming throughout her confrontation with Jake. Therefore, she also had no idea that the information it had gathered was being stored, filed away in the memory banks of the Deveraux College's master computer, perfectly preserved for later, for an unspecified and unknowable date in the future. When it might be needed.

Lori shook her head. Maybe she'd expected too much from her relationships so far, invested too much of herself in them. It seemed to her she hadn't got much in return for her investment. Maybe it was time to avoid serious emotional entanglements. Less of the *lurve*, more of the fun. There'd be fewer disappointments that way. Less pain. It might even help her forget Jake. Eventually.

She got to her feet with purpose, like someone called on to receive a prize. When Agent Angel Blue returned to her Californian placement, things were going to change.

ONE

Ninety degrees again, and if she had any sense she'd never go anywhere else. The sun was scorching a golden hole in the Californian sky. The beach was a dazzling curve of yellow and the sea a sparkling blue.

Surf up.

Lying on her board and paddling with strong, supple strokes, Lori felt the wave nudging, propelling her forward. With a whoop of excitement, she jumped to her feet. Instant balance, precise balance as the wave swelled beneath her and bore her board upwards. She let the ocean rush her towards shore, the distribution of her weight keeping the surfboard's nose above water. She twisted to the right, slicing across the wave like an oversized knife. Then twisted to the left, her leaning and weight adjustments impeccable, her long hair streaming out behind her. The sea was at her mercy. She could do whatever she liked with it.

These days many surfers used smartboards, computer-controlled so that while their manoeuvres were impressive, the skill was the machine's, not the rider's.

Lori preferred to surf 'naked', as the jargon went, just her and the hurtling sea in harmony. You didn't need technology for that. Besides, the virtual library at Carmody's allowed her to practise her moves on every major surfing beach in the world under every type of conditions. And practice, as everyone knew whether or not they were secret agents in the employ of the Deveraux organisation, made only one thing.

Lori was *it* as she zigzagged imperiously, dramatically towards the beach.

Too close to the beach. A pity. It meant she'd have to leave the wave. Lori often thought that riding each new wave was like the first kiss with a new boyfriend – you never knew exactly what to expect, but it always turned out to be a thrill and it was always over too soon. Boys had one major advantage over waves though: you could always go back for more. Lori's wave was about to disappear for ever.

She shifted her weight backwards, swivelled her board in the water as the wave disintegrated entirely into surf. She stepped off into warm water. Choices: paddle back out and catch another wave, or stroll ashore and grab a cold drink. Her small clutch of admirers made her mind up for her.

'That was great. That was really great.'

'Cool moves, Lori. You sure know how to handle the surf.'

Lori grinned. She doubted she'd even have to *buy* the drink.

Most of the half dozen boys who moved in to congratulate her were surfers, too. She knew their faces and some of their names, though most of *them* owned smartboards.

They'd been keen for her to demonstrate her technique. She'd been keen to show it off. It was six months since the Lorenzo mission and she was down to thinking of Jake just once a day. It was like giving up smoking. Having so much attention helped . . . sort of.

'Thirsty work, though,' she hinted to the crowd. 'I could do with a drink.'

'Let me get you a Coke or something.' The boy who offered was behind her left shoulder. She hadn't noticed him there, though she remembered him vaguely. He was sandy-haired and pasty-faced, as if he'd spent his whole life avoiding the sun.

'Thanks,' Lori smiled. 'That's very kind of you, Kelvin.'

'It's Calvin,' the boy corrected. 'My name is Calvin.'

'Oh, I'm sorry.' Lori persisted with the smile. 'You look like a Kelvin to me.'

'No . . . *Cal*vin . . .'

'Who cares?' A tanned surfer stepped in, guided Lori by the elbow. 'Let's *all* have a drink. Then we can talk about what we're going to do tonight.'

Lori laughed, allowed herself to be escorted to the beach bar. The sun was on her back, the boys were at her feet, and life was good.

```
IGC MONITORING FILE US1
SUBJECT: PRESIDENT OF THE UNITED STATES OF AMERICA
         FROM FOX-PUTIN NETWORK COVERAGE
```

President Graveney Westwood was in bullish mood today as he arrived in Los Angeles on the first leg of his Californian tour. The president will be attending a number of public functions as well as meeting leading business and political figures privately to lobby for support for the second stage of his Earth Protection Initiative (EPI). He may well need to be at the peak of his powers of persuasion. The malfunction of the Guardian Star space station, intended as the cornerstone of EPI, and for reasons still not revealed, remains fresh in the country's mind, and may be of particular concern to those from whom donations towards its successors might be expected.

At a press conference, following the routine airport security measures of a strip search and a DNA confirmation test, President Westwood was optimistic. 'Of course folk'll want to make contributions to EPI,' he said. 'EPI is a hell of a good idea, I've always said so. And folk want to be associated with hell of a good ideas. Sure they do. They'll be signing cheques before I ask 'em. Or who knows, the guns in the sky could be turned on *them*. Heh, heh. I'm joking, of course. But it *is* the solemn duty of every American citizen to do whatever he can to combat the scourge of terrorism that tragically and traumatically is still with us today.'

The President was then asked about the rumours that had recently been leaked to the media involving a possible assassination plot against him.

'I take as little notice of those kinds of rumours as I do of the pollsters who wrote me off in 2064,' he replied with a hearty laugh.

'You all should know by now, you can't get rid of Graveney Westwood so easily. Now if you'll excuse me, I have a schedule to keep and nobody and nothing, certainly not scurrilous rumours about assassination threats, are gonna stop me.'

'What do you mean, still no concrete intelligence?' President Graveney Westwood circled the desk nervously, gnawing at his lower lip and performing invisible origami with his fingers. 'So find some, get some, do whatever it is you turkeys in the bureau *do* to keep this nation safe for democracy. There are three living presidents in retirement right now, Quilby, and I intend to be number four, do you understand what I'm saying?'

'Yes, sir. Perfectly, sir.' The voice from over the speaker-phone sounded suitably chastened. 'I'll get straight back on it, sir, personally.'

'See that you do, Quilby, or else you can look forward to spending the rest of your career in the bureau as a *janitor*.'

'Yes, sir, Mr President, sir.'

Westwood turned to his vice-president, the only other occupant of the office, as Quilby rang off. 'What do these FBI guys get paid for, huh, Gayle? The way they limp from lead to lead, anyone'd think they wanted to get me shot. By the way, do you think this new bullet-proof vest I'm wearing makes me look fat?'

'Of course not, Mr President,' Gayle Steinwitz said soothingly.

'And these windows,' Westwood eyed them apprehensively, 'they're triple-reinforced glasteel like I requested?'

'*Exactly* as you requested, Mr President.' Gayle Steinwitz, tall, elegant and fifty, but looking ten years younger even without facial reconstruction, was more than used to her superior's paranoia. She'd lived with it every day since their first election in 2060, and now she had only two more years to put up with it. Just as well. If anything, since the Guardian Star episode a couple of years back, Westwood had been getting worse. 'Do you think we could concentrate on some business, sir?'

Westwood had sneaked over to the wall, had crouched down and was tentatively lifting his head above the window-sill, like a soldier in the trenches. 'Let 'em try. Let the terrorists try, huh, Gayle? They can't get me in here, can they? All the time I stay in here I'm safe.'

'Sir? Business?'

Westwood regarded his vice-president enviously. 'How come nothing ever seems to worry you, Gayle?'

It was true. Steinwitz was generally known among the White House staff as the Iceberg. She supposed her renowned coolness under pressure was at least partly due to her distant Scandinavian ancestry. Wherever it came from, it had many commentators tipping her for the only office in the land higher than the one she currently held. Whether she heeded such comments, however, nobody could tell.

'You can let me in on it, Gayle,' Westwood was continuing. 'I'm the president. What's your secret?'

'Work, Mr President,' revealed Gayle, 'and plenty of it. Then I don't have time to think of anything else. And talking of work, we really must look at tomorrow's schedule again . . .'

'T'hell with tomorrow's schedule, Gayle,' scoffed

Westwood, 'and the day after that's, *and* the day after that's. D'you think I'm stepping out there –' indicating the world at large – 'with no triple-reinforced glasteel windows to protect me while my boys in the FBI are picking up threats against my life?'

'But you told the reporters at the press conference . . .'

'I told them what they wanted to hear,' said the president. 'That's what a politician does, Gayle, haven't you learned that yet? And now I want *our* press people to tell 'em that President Westwood's come over all sick and bad and though he valiantly tried to raise himself from his bed, his doctors insisted he stay there for at least three days. And in the meantime, the President's engagements will be fulfilled by Vice-President Gayle Steinwitz. You don't mind, honey, do you?'

'What's to mind?' Gayle said coolly.

'That's just peachy. I knew you'd understand.' There was a knock at the door. 'Come right in, whoever you are.'

It was a woman in her early thirties with a snub nose, absolutely no make-up and short black hair that seemed to have been scribbled on her head with a pen. She had a clipboard and a sheaf of papers under her arm. Ms Debbie Hunter, the president's therapist. The president's very much in demand therapist, Gayle Steinwitz thought.

'Debbie.' Westwood's mood brightened at once. 'Is it that time already?' Ms Hunter assured him that it was. 'Well, if you can excuse us, Gayle, there's a lot I need to put my mind at ease about and Debbie's the only one who can help me. Don't forget to tell the press people what we decided, will you?'

'No, sir,' said Gayle, standing and making her way,

elegantly and without fluster, to the door. 'I won't forget anything.' As Debbie Hunter slipped into her chair while the seat was no doubt still warm. As she heard behind her before the door clicked closed: 'Debbie, I've been having these dreams . . .'

Gayle Steinwitz stood in the corridor. She was as still and impassive as, well, an iceberg. Two more years to endure a day-to-day working relationship with Graveney Westwood. Right now that seemed an insuperable length of time. Two more years.

Unless, of course, something happened to the president in the meantime . . .

The students had gone to shower and change. Their mothers had come to collect them. The lesson was over.

Good thing, too, chafed Lori Angel – *Miss* Lori as her younger charges called her – tapping her foot impatiently in the studio and longing to do a little bit of showering and changing herself. The clock was ticking towards tonight. She couldn't head for *Metro* in a leotard as sweaty as *this* leotard. She needed to do something with her hair as well. Lori examined herself in the mirror walls of the dance studio. Everything else, on the other hand, was looking fine.

'Excuse me. Ms Angel?' It was a mother at the door.

'You've come to the right place,' Lori admitted, donning her official smile. She should have done a runner sooner. What did the woman want?

'I'd just like a word, if I may. I'm Eleanor Kiley. You take my daughter Chrissie for ballet and moon mood.'

'I do indeed,' said Lori, shaking Ms Kiley's hand. 'Chrissie's doing very well. She's showing real potential.'

'That's what I wanted a word about, Ms Angel.'

Uh oh, Lori groaned inwardly. Complaint incoming. Dive for cover. Or at least let it be brief. Brad was waiting. 'Really?' She tactfully tried to guide the older woman towards the exit. 'Let's walk while we talk.'

'Yes. I have to say, Ms Angel, I had significant reservations about sending Chrissie to Carmody's at the beginning, especially when I learned that she would not be taught by Ms Carmody herself but by a rather younger and less experienced dance instructor. You.'

'Yes, well, I'm afraid Ms Carmody does very little teaching these days, Ms Kiley,' said Lori. Here it came. Pushy mother was removing darling daughter from the school.

'But I have to say I was absolutely wrong to be concerned,' Eleanor Kiley smiled. 'You've done wonders for Chrissie's dancing, Ms Angel, marvels, and more importantly than that, you've boosted her self-confidence no end.'

'That's nice of you to say so,' winced Lori. How wrong could she have been?

'Yes indeed. You may not know it, Ms Angel, but you've become very much a role model, not only to Chrissie but to the other girls as well. They all want to be like you.'

'They do?'

'You set them such a *good* example.'

Lori thought about all the partying she'd done lately. 'Do I?'

'You're a fine teacher, Ms Angel, I just wanted to tell you that.' They were at the doors to the street. Lori saw Chrissie Kiley waiting outside. The girl's mother patted her hand. 'A fine teacher and a good person. You should be proud of yourself.'

'Thank you,' Lori said as the woman took her leave. 'Thanks a lot.' But for some reason she didn't feel so proud.

She shook her head. No time for self-analysis now. She just had to close down the studio, then she could get ready to hit the clubs with Brad.

But Luanne Carmody was waiting in the dance studio. Owner of and senior teacher at the Carmody Dance Academy, Los Angeles, California, Luanne Carmody was tall, black, striking and blind. Blind, but able to see, thanks to the ultra-sensitive optical implants that had been screwed into place in the ruined sockets of her original eyes, requiring her to wear thick dark glasses at all times and earning her the nickname Shades from her students. Students who little guessed her main source of employment. Luanne Carmody, Angel Blue's field handler.

Because the Carmody Dance Academy did not exist for its own sake. It was there to provide a cover occupation for Lori in her capacity as Spy High graduate and secret agent. That was why she lived on the premises, why Luanne Carmody did so, too. That was why the smart studio where she and her field handler now stood would at a word convert to a holo-gym – exchanging dance steps for combat moves, and with no accompanying music. Other rooms in the school had similar hidden talents. It wasn't everywhere that kept SkyBikes in the shower block.

'Lessons finished for the day, Lori?' said Luanne.

'Just about.'

'*Dance* lessons, I mean.'

'What?' Lori didn't like the emphasis in Luanne's words.

'I feel *you* might benefit from a little more target practice with the *shuriken*. Your martial arts performances have been a little inconsistent lately.'

'Do you think?' It was the last thing Lori wanted. She wanted to be selecting her outfit for tonight, not throwing sharpened metal stars at bits of wood. She'd done her specified amount of spy training that morning. Where was Shades coming from expecting more? 'Actually, Luanne, can we kind of give it a miss until our combat session tomorrow? I mean, I can disable an attacker in six different ways with my little finger already. The *shuriken* can wait, can't they? I've got a date that can't. This *is* my own time now.'

'Technically, of course, you're correct, Lori,' said Luanne. 'This *is* your own time, and far be it for me to come between you and your social life. I used to have one myself. But we could be faced with an emergency situation at *any* time, you know that, and we need to be ready. Inconsistencies in training could adversely affect performance where it matters, in the field. You going that extra mile now could save your life later.'

She was right, of course. Deep down, Lori knew it. Her insistence on what she called the three tees necessary for a spy's survival – training, training and training – was what made Luanne Carmody such a successful field handler. No Deveraux agent assigned to her care had ever returned from a mission with anything more life-threatening than a flesh wound. Shades had personal experience of disasters on active duty: she'd lost her eyes on the same mission that had cost Lori's old Senior Tutor his legs. She'd sworn that no similar fate would befall her charges.

But *knowing* Luanne was right and *acting* on it were different things. And Lori was aware of that, too. 'Luanne,' she said, 'tonight's really special to me. Can we *really* not postpone that extra mile until the morning? Then I'll go two, I promise.'

Shades regarded her levelly. If she'd still had eyes, and they hadn't been shielded by dark glasses, Lori would have seen disappointment in them. 'It's your choice, Lori.'

'Cool. So we'll train tomorrow. I'll be here early. Have a good evening, Luanne.' She turned to get out before Shades could add one last thing.

'One last thing.' Too slow. 'Not so long ago you'd have been suggesting extra sessions yourself, Lori, you wouldn't have needed me to prompt you. And you sure wouldn't have been putting boys and clubbing ahead of your Deveraux responsibilities . . .'

'I'm not actually doing that now, Luanne,' Lori sought to defend herself.

'Up to about six months ago, in fact.' The field handler continued undeterred. 'Up to the Lorenzo mission with Jake Daly. You haven't been quite the same since then. At least, that's how it looks to me.'

'Look harder, then,' Lori snapped, and then remembered herself and was stung with guilt. 'I'm sorry, Luanne. I shouldn't have said that.'

Luanne waved the offence away. 'Something on your mind, Lori? You know you can always talk to me. It doesn't have to be spying business. Teenage business can be just as thorny. And I'm your mentor as well as your field handler. Least, I'd like to be if you'll let me.'

'Thanks, Luanne. I appreciate it. Maybe . . .' Sometimes, Lori thought, Shades saw things as they truly were more sharply than those with eyes. 'Maybe another time. I've got to go. Got to get ready. Bye.'

She ran all the way to her rooms as if someone or something was chasing her.

There was no moon tonight and precious few stars, and he was in a part of town that seemed to be well behind with its electricity payments, but Simon Grey, formerly Simon Macey of Solo Team at the Deveraux College, might have wished for his surroundings to be even blacker. Your chances of eluding those who wanted to kill you were always improved in the dark.

He kept close to the sides of buildings, hugged the shadows like girls he'd loved for a long time. Thought of Lori. She was the nearest. It would have to be her. If his situation wasn't so desperate, he'd have smiled.

There was a rattle from the murk behind him. Simon whirled and fired his sleepshot, heard the scurrying of unseen paws: scavengers among the rubbish, not human pursuit. There probably wasn't anything human here, not among these tenements – desolate and apparently deserted, as though the streets had been evacuated ahead of some terrible disaster. But there was no way for Simon to be sure.

They'd caught him unawares. How they'd located his apartment, rented under a false name, he didn't know. If he'd been slack he was paying for it. He'd been watching videvision, one of those old James Bond movies with the guy whose accent he couldn't understand. They were always good for a laugh.

He should have been watching the window. And the door.

Like he should be watching behind him now. And ahead. In every direction. If only he had a radar visor. But their attack had been so sudden. If he hadn't neglected to remove his wristbands he wouldn't even have his sleepshot, he'd be weaponless. As it was he had no communicator, no means of summoning back-up.

Reaching Lori was his only option.

Simon eased stealthily forward. He'd escaped similar predicaments countless times back at Spy High. In virtual reality, of course, but the principle was the same. Attune your senses to the dark. Look for the slightest stirring of the night, like a ripple in a black pool. Listen for the smallest of nocturnal sounds. Never turn your back on a shadow.

And was that something there – someone? – standing where the streetlight should have shone? Soundless, motionless, but surely a denser kind of darkness, a more solid kind of shape. Was it one of them? Why didn't it make its move?

He'd enjoyed the old stealth modules back at Spy High. They'd been a bit like the games of hide and seek he'd played as a boy.

He raised his arm to shoot.

A cackle, again from behind him. Again he whirled. Saw the tramp in time. Relaxed.

Never turn your back on a shadow.

Slow to respond. Stupid. Slow. She was beside him. She was on him. As close as his own breath.

He'd not seen her before. He'd not see her again.

A flash of something silver in the gloom. A knife.

All right, hand on heart, if she had to be honest Brad was a bit of a lame date. A bit like Josh and Luke – in fact everyone she'd gone out with since Jake. Egos on legs. Personalities as empty as a club after closing-time. They were like books with colourful, dynamic covers that made you want to pick them up off the shelf, but when you opened them to start reading, the pages were blank. Or if not, the writing was very simple and very big. Lori supposed it didn't really matter. To extend the analogy, you could always put a book you didn't want *back* on the shelf and select another. There were plenty of attractive covers to choose from.

And it was sort of fun to be out with a different guy every night. The avoiding emotional entanglements kind of fun. The no strings kind of good time. Loud music. Bright lights. And no relationship issues to worry about.

So why was she in the ladies room locked in a cubicle? Was it just because her date danced like he was still on a surfboard? Whatever, the two girls who came in obviously didn't know she was still there. They couldn't have done. Otherwise they wouldn't have been talking about her quite so openly.

'You see that surfer chick's here again tonight.'

'She's here *every* night. Got a season ticket. See who she's with?'

'Brad Spencer. Mr Bland and Brainless 2066. A perfect match if you ask me.

'Well, it'll be somebody else tomorrow anyway. I

reckon she's got a list of all the guys in LA and she's ticking 'em off one by one.'

'She should be halfway through by now.'

'I don't know, though. Girls like her give the rest of us a bad name. Makes boys think we're easy.'

'So this is you making a stand for females everywhere, is it? Nothing to do with jealousy. Long blonde hair? Perfect figure?'

'Looks don't last. If all she's got going for her is a cheesy smile and a fit body, she's even sadder than I thought and one day she'll wake up with nothing.'

'You hope.'

'I *know*. Now are you gonna lend me some of your lipstick or what?'

That was one way to ruin an evening. Lori sat silently in the cubicle while the two girls finished refreshing their make-up. Her Spy High memory training meant that she was expert at remembering huge chunks of conversation almost verbatim. It was a skill she would have gladly abandoned at that moment.

Easy. Not a word she ever expected to be used in connection with her. Not justified, either, but part of her could see why other people might think so. She'd never done anything she shouldn't have with the guys she'd dated. All she'd wanted was a bit of fun. And no strings.

Maybe it was time to go home.

But even that wasn't going to be easy.

'Oh, great,' she groaned. He was outside in the corridor. Must have seen her go in. Not Brad, but the sandy-haired and pasty-faced guy from the beach. He didn't look happy.

'What's my name?' he demanded awkwardly. 'Do you remember my name, Lori?'

'Of course I do.' Though Lori was beginning to wish she'd never seen him. Never met any of them. 'It's Calvin, isn't it? Nice to see you, Calvin. Now if you'll excuse me . . .'

It seemed he wouldn't. He stepped across her path. Music throbbed in the background like a headache. 'That's right. That's good. *Cal*vin. But you should have remembered this afternoon.'

'That's right. I should have. I will tomorrow. Now . . .' *Get out of my way.*

'You can make it up to me. You can dance with me.'

'I don't think so, Calvin, thanks for the offer. I've really got to go. I'm not feeling well.' Wasn't *that* the truth.

He didn't seem impressed. 'First you don't remember my name. Then you don't want to dance with me. But I *love* you, Lori.'

So there it was. Full-on nightmare. 'No, you don't, Calvin. Now if I can just . . .' But he moved to block her every time.

'You're the most amazing girl I've ever seen.'

'No, I'm not, Calvin, or if I am you need to get out more. And please, I'm warning you . . .'

'Lori . . .' He reached out his hand.

'Get out of my way!' And she took it. And in a move that would have been very much to Shades Carmody's satisfaction, she threw him. He landed on his back, winded but with nothing broken. 'I'm flattered, Calvin, honestly I am, but let me tell you, I'm not the girl for you. Right now I'm not sure I'm the girl for anyone.'

The only consolation for Lori's present mood was this: at least the night couldn't get any worse.

She could have caught a cab but decided to walk back to

the school and her bed. The notoriously treacherous streets of Los Angeles held no fear for Angel Blue. In fact, Lori might have welcomed a mugger or three jumping out at her from an alleyway. Unlike with Calvin, she'd have felt no pressure to pull her punches. Or her kicks.

By the time she was approaching Carmody's she was beginning to feel a little better. Let other people talk. They obviously had nothing better to do. They didn't know her. They didn't know who she truly was. If they thought she was an easy target for every boy with biceps, that only proved how successful she'd been in establishing a plausible and persuasive cover identity. She ought to be glad.

Ought to be.

Her foot came away from the pavement with the sound of a sticking plaster being removed. She'd inadvertently trodden in something icky. A kid's discarded chewing gum, probably. She slipped her shoe off to look. Hoped it wasn't ruined. These were her favourite shoes, horribly expensive, and she couldn't exactly hop to parties and clubs on just one of them.

It was a false alarm, anyway. The substance clinging to the bottom of her shoe wasn't gum. It was redder than gum, and before it had started to dry had once been more liquid.

Anyone who hadn't graduated from Spy High might have thought paint or nail varnish or ketchup, but Lori's training meant she recognised blood when she saw it. And where there was blood, someone had to be bleeding.

Metres from her secret base of operations. Coincidence? She'd been taught that there was no such thing, only patterns that had yet to be understood.

Lori slid her shoe back on and darted towards the school building. The entrance at the top of the steps. The dark pit where the doors were.

He lunged out at her but she didn't scream. He clutched for her and he said her name but both fingers and voice were failing, lacking strength. He pitched forward and fell to the steps. And she knew him.

'Simon!'

She crouched beside him instantly, turning him over, lifting his head. His shirt front was stained red as if he'd spilled a glass of red wine. But he hadn't.

'Simon, what . . .? We've got to get you inside.'

Lori scoured the surrounding darkness, the buildings that seemed to have turned their backs declaring that they had nothing to do with any of this.

What if his assailant was still watching?

'No . . . Lori . . . no good.' It was white, Simon's face, like he was already a ghost, like he was physically preparing to be talked about in the past tense. 'I reached you . . . at least I did that . . .'

'We've got a meditech facility here, Simon. Let's just get inside.'

The last of his strength gripped her there. '. . . tell you . . . have to tell you . . .'

'What? Simon. Tell me what?'

A word. She thought she heard it.

'. . . assassination . . .'

TWO

The Deveraux College, some way north of Boston, Massachusetts, was not like other schools. Its reunions were not like other school reunions. They only took place when someone had died.

They took place quite frequently.

The class of 2064, those who had studied, trained and graduated with the late Simon Macey, those who had returned from across the world to commemorate one of the Fallen were gathered in the Hall of Heroes. Simon's remains were not with them. His body had been despatched to his parents together with a lie, that he had been killed by a mugger in a random act of street violence. The truth was spelled out in the plaque granted pride of place in this revered chamber: 'Dedicated to the graduates of the Deveraux College. To those who risk their lives for the sake of tomorrow.'

The truth, often necessarily, concealed by a falsehood. Like the gothic façade of the Devereaux College – a seemingly select and slightly stuffy educational establishment, it was in actuality an ultra-modern training facility for the next generation of world-saving secret agents.

Lori glanced at her former team-mates while they waited for Jonathan Deveraux to speak. They were all there – Eddie, Cally, Bex. And Ben. And Jake. She'd elected to stand as far from Jake as she could. She didn't want any friction between the two of them to taint an occasion that should be about the fallen.

Although Simon had never, if she was truthful, been her favourite person. In their first year of training when her team and Simon's had been competing against each other for the Sherlock Shield, he'd pretended to be attracted to her in order to win her confidence and use her to betray her partners. The scheme would have worked, too, but for Jake. Lori smiled thinly, wondering if things would go the same way now. But what did it matter anyway? It seemed so long ago already. So Simon Macey had had a deceitful and manipulative streak in him. So what? He was gone now, and he'd died striving to protect countless people he'd never met. She tried to think of that. Focus on the good.

The truth, often necessarily, concealed by a falsehood.

The voice of Jonathan Deveraux, the college's founder, boomed through the Hall of Heroes like the voice of God. His austere, handsome features appeared in holo-form, the iron-grey hair, the resolute eyes, the square and jutting chin, hovering in the air, transmitted directly from his own quarters, the topmost floor of the College. He talked about Simon, and how the body might have perished but the spirit would live on. Lori supposed that Jonathan Deveraux knew all about living on after the body had perished. *His* had gone the way of all flesh years ago, but his mind had been saved, salvaged, downloaded, computerised. He'd outlast every one of them. And he was talking about Simon being immortalised too, in the memories of his fellow graduates and in the annals of Spy High. Students yet to be born would come here, he said, and they would learn of him and they would see him.

As if on cue, a second hologram appeared, materialising above the plinth that bore the name of Simon Macey like a tombstone. It was dazzling, golden. A figure of light that was larger than life, better than life, more perfect and fulfilled. Simon Macey, strong and ideal, his eyes searching the far horizons, going beyond the pettiness and paltriness of this world.

'Goodbye, Simon,' she whispered.

'So, how are things generally, Lori? I mean, other than today.' The memorial ceremony was over and the mourners had dispersed. Lori, Ben and Cally had headed to the rec room. The latter was ordering drinks from the counter, allowing her companions a few minutes alone together. It was just like old times.

'Oh, fine, Ben. Things are fine. Thanks.'

'Only I'd heard – and stop me if you think I'm getting intrusive – I'd heard there were problems between you and Jake. Did I hear right?'

'Yes. It's true. Jake and I are history.' Just like *you* and I are history, Lori thought. That was the thing about history. It was always repeating itself.

'Yeah? I'm sorry.'

'Are you?' She scrutinised Ben Stanton closely. He was more gorgeous than ever, she had to admit. Fair where Jake was dark, aristocratic where Jake was wild.

He was like a male version of herself. Small wonder everyone had expected the two of them to become an item. Small wonder few had anticipated her split from him, especially when she'd then started seeing Jake. And Ben for one had not taken their break-up well. She wondered how genuinely sympathetic he was now. 'You're really sorry, Ben?'

'Sure I am. For you, Lori. If splitting up with Daly hurt you. I haven't got much time for Jake, you know I never had, but you also know how I used to feel about you . . .'

'Used to, Ben?' It sounded more suggestive than she'd intended (but then he *was* more gorgeous than ever).

'*Used* to.' He smiled. 'We had something special, didn't we, even if it finished, how shall I put it, *untidily*?'

'Untidily sounds about right,' Lori laughed.

'But in the end I wished you well with Jake and I meant it and yes, I really am sorry it hasn't worked out. But I've found something special again, Lori, and this time I'm holding on to it.'

He glanced meaningfully towards the dreadlocked figure of Cally, who was approaching fast and holding on to a tray. Another unexpected match, Lori thought. Or maybe it was just that Bond Team had been kind of crazy and mixed up from the very start.

Lori didn't want to add to it now. As Cally put three drinks down, she stood up. Three was a crowd.

'You're not going, are you, Lo?' Cally was disappointed. 'We've got loads to talk about.'

'Sorry, Cal, I've just remembered. Mr Deveraux's got some things he wants to talk about, too. Tell you what, split my drink between the two of you. Catch you later.'

Cally watched her former team-mate rush off. 'What's with her?' she said.

Lori reviewed Simon's files during the flight back to California. She'd been allocated a private Deveraux jet, so there was plenty of room for her to spread out. She supposed she shouldn't have been surprised when Jonathan Deveraux had assigned her to complete Simon Macey's final mission, bearing in mind not only that she was the organisation's West Coast agent – the region designated Blue – but also that poor Simon had made his last contact with her.

Assassination, he'd said. As far as it went, that made sense to Jonathan Deveraux. Simon's codename was Grey. Unlike other operatives' codenames, Grey did not relate to a part of the world but to a type of assignment. It was Simon's job to monitor intelligence and from the cacophonous chaos of information that Spy High received on a daily, even hourly basis, select and identify any credible terrorist threats. When he was killed, Deveraux told Lori, Simon had been investigating a possible plot against the life of the president himself. He was in Los Angeles because Graveney Westwood was in Los Angeles. The fact that he *had* been killed, and with the word *assassination* on his lips, very much suggested that such a plot *did* exist, and that an attempt on the president might be imminent. The apartment building where Simon had been staying had been razed to the ground, his original files either taken or destroyed. Like all intelligence agents in the field, however, he'd copied them to Spy High automatically. Lori's first task was to sift through them. Her second was to find a lead, either to whoever had murdered Simon or whoever was planning to murder the president.

She wasn't getting very far. Simon's records were clear and orderly, almost as if they were lined up ready for inspection, but simply seemed to confirm what Jonathan Deveraux had already told her. There was nothing to alert her secret agent senses. The plane had already crossed the Mississippi and she had only Simon's anomaly file left to read. It was unlikely, but maybe she'd find something useful in there.

Intelligence agents always kept an anomaly file, because where established, everyday lines of inquiry failed, sometimes the abnormal or the unexpected or the just plain weird might succeed. Into an anomaly file agents would feed a number of key words relevant to the case they were pursuing. Deveraux's computers and the Intelligence Gathering Centre itself would then carry out regular data sweeps searching for the slightest fragment of information connected to the key words. The process was a kind of high-tech lateral thinking.

Simon had keyed in a number of searches: presidential assassination attempts, Graveney Westwood, American terrorist suspects, anti-Westwood demonstrations, security services and agencies (prioritise anti-terrorist activities), radical publications, videvision chat shows, immigration records, a lot more besides. Lori was surprised the laptop's memory could handle it all. Hers certainly couldn't. She instructed her machine to organise the information by date of inclusion, starting with the most recent additions and working backwards.

She didn't actually have very far backwards to go. The item was dated the day before Simon's death. It was perfect anomaly file material. Instinctively, she knew it was what she'd been looking for.

By the time they landed at the airport, a wheelless was waiting to drive Lori to her interview with Mrs Susan Stockdale.

'A little young for a reporter, aren't you, Miss Angel?' said Mrs Stockdale, leading her into a conservatively but tastefully decorated lounge.

'News is a young person's profession these days, Mrs Stockdale,' Lori breezed, in what she hoped was a thrusting, go-getting, ambitious kind of way.

'Yes, well, it's a young person's *world* too, I suppose. Pass forty these days and they think you're ready for your pension. I'll be fifty next year. I expect they'll want to be measuring me for my box.'

'Oh, I doubt that, Mrs Stockdale,' Lori beamed disarmingly.

'No? They already must think I'm senile. Or crazy. The police obviously didn't believe a word I said. They haven't got back to me or anything. The only person who's shown the slightest interest is you, Miss Angel.' She frowned slightly. 'How did you find out, incidentally? The only people I've told are the police.'

'Oh, we have our contacts at WLMX, Mrs Stockdale,' winked Lori. And a direct link from Spy High to every police precinct in the country. 'And my producer found your story very interesting indeed.'

Mrs Stockdale seemed mollified. 'Well, then I'm glad somebody in this godforsaken country of ours still has some sense. Coffee, Miss Angel? It's fresh.'

While her hostess fetched it, Lori quickly analysed the

room. Furnishings and choice of ornaments, decoration, all provided clues to the personality of their owner. The fabrics, traditional. The colours, muted and respectable. The paintings on the wall, Norman Rockwell prints. The magazines on the coffee table, *American Life* and *Yesterday Illustrated*. Susan Stockdale was clearly a solid, patriotic citizen, perhaps a little unhealthily nostalgic, perhaps not entirely at her ease with the 2060s, but certainly not somebody prone to flights of fantasy or sudden hallucinations.

The photograph, given pride of place on the heavy mahogany sideboard, of a stern commanding man with close-cropped hair and a military chin drew Lori's gaze.

'Yes, this is him,' Mrs Stockdale said in answer to the question a few moments later. 'Dane. My husband. It was the last photograph taken of him before he died . . . sorry, before I *thought* he died.'

'When was that, Mrs Stockdale?' Lori asked, accepting the framed photo as the older woman handed it to her like a priest giving communion.

'Three years ago. March third, 2063. He was forty-eight years old.'

'Can you tell me what Dane did for a living?'

'He worked for the government. Something to do with taxes. He never liked to talk work at home. Said most of what he did was dull. But, he said, it was important, too. It was taxes that led to the downfall of Al Capone, not men with guns. He always said that. My Dane, he believed in the citizen's right to bear arms and protect himself, but he wouldn't have hurt a fly.'

'I'm sure you're right, Mrs Stockdale,' lied Lori. She looked into Dane Stockdale's brown eyes. They gave nothing away. Particularly not that his actual line of work had had nothing to do with taxes but everything to do with terrorism and its prevention. According to Deveraux intelligence, Dane Stockdale had been a member of TAG, the Terrorism Action Group, a covert government agency set up to counter terrorist threats from within America itself. That was how, once Mrs Stockdale's local police precinct had logged their report of what she'd tried to persuade them, Dane Stockdale had found his way on to Simon Macey's anomaly file.

'Mrs Stockdale,' said Lori, 'would you mind telling me *how* Dane died?'

'How it *appeared* he had,' insisted his widow. 'Yes, if you like. It was a wheelless crash. Dane had been attending a function upstate. No other vehicles were involved but the weather was terrible – a freak storm with near impossible driving conditions. He shouldn't have been out in them but he wanted to get home to me. He lost control of his wheelless and plunged down a ravine and was killed. At least, everyone *thought* he'd been killed. And why not? I had to identify the body. I *saw* the body. The wheelless hadn't burst into flames or anything, that doesn't happen with these magnetic engines, does it? I saw Dane and I could recognise him easily and it *was* him. I was there when they locked the coffin down. I was there when they lowered it into the ground and when the earth was shovelled . . . aren't you taking notes on any of this, Miss Angel?'

'Ah, no. No. Not right now,' Lori admitted. 'If it's all right with you, Mrs Stockdale. I just see this as a pre-liminary meeting. If my producer decides to run with the story – and I'm sure he will – I'll come back with a camera crew. At a convenient time, of course.'

'Of course,' said Susan Stockdale, a little frostily now. 'If you've finished with Dane's photograph . . .'

Lori thought she'd better push on. 'Thank you, it's a very good . . . Excellent coffee, too, really hot . . . So tell me what happened when you saw your husband last week, Mrs Stockdale . . .'

'Very well,' she said primly. 'I was visiting my sister in Sacramento. She's only recently moved there and I'd never been before either. We were shopping, I forget the name of the mall. I can't imagine it's important. What is important is what happened when my sister and I were having lunch in a nice little café. I was looking around for the waitress when I saw this man standing outside, peering in through the window. I realised I knew him immediately, but *exactly* who he was didn't register until I'd almost looked away again. You know how it can be if you pass somebody familiar unexpectedly in the street. Then it hit me. It was Dane, my own husband. It was Dane alive again. And I cried out, of course, and snapped my attention back to him, and he was still there –' she shook the photograph as if providing proof – 'looking like he does here, the same. And this time he saw me too and he recognised me, I could see it in his eyes. But he didn't come closer. He didn't come in. He backed away.'

'So what did you do?' pressed Lori.

'I got up. I must have been unsteady on my feet. I knocked a glass to the floor, I heard it smash.' Susan Stockdale was reliving the event. 'I heard my sister calling after me but I was crying out his name. And I ran from the café as he was walking away quickly, deliberately, as if he didn't want me to catch up with him. And there were people all around, so many people crowding between us, and I shouted and screamed for him, but he didn't hear me or he didn't listen, and then he was lost among the people. And then someone was seizing my arm and it was the waitress from the café, demanding I pay for the meal or she would call security.'

'Did you explain to your sister, Mrs Stockdale?' Lori asked.

'Oh, yes,' the woman bridled, 'but she just told me to take a nap and a pill. Sarah doesn't believe I've ever properly recovered from the shock of Dane's death – apparent death. But I have. I'm of sound mind. I know what I saw, *who* I saw. That's why when I came back home I reported it to the police. I wanted Dane to be registered as a missing person. I wanted them to find him. Because, don't you see, Miss Angel, Dane can't have been dead when they put him in that coffin after all. He must have been in a coma, in a trance that the doctors missed. And then, later, he must have awoken and got out of the coffin somehow and then closed the lid again and we must have buried an empty box while Dane was still alive. That makes sense. That could happen, couldn't it? And he must have lost his memory because of the trauma of what had happened to him which would explain why . . . for three years . . . But why didn't he come to me when he saw me through the window, Miss Angel? Why didn't he do that?'

'I'm afraid I don't know,' said Lori.

She understood why the police hadn't believed Susan Stockdale's fantastic tale of a resurrected husband. Lori, on the other hand, was prepared to give her the benefit of the doubt. A coffined and comatose Dane suddenly recovering and finding his way out, she had little truck with *that* particular scenario – and neither did Shades Carmody following Lori's debrief – but a body *other* than Dane Stockdale's being deposited in the coffin in the first place, a body physically reconstructed to *look* like Dane Stockdale's, that was an altogether more plausible possibility.

The obvious question, of course, was why. On her return to the dance school Lori had hacked into the TAG computer. Stockdale was simply registered deceased. Official contacts with the agency via Deveraux confirmed it. No undercover operations requiring its participants to fake their own death had ever been undertaken by the Terrorism Action Group nor were envisaged for the future. Even in the dark corners of the espionage world, dead was dead was dead. Yeah, right, scoffed Lori, remembering her mission against the crazed Dr Frankenstein, and Jennifer Chen, her dead friend whom the mad doctor had made live again. Anyway, if the records offered no clues, they still had one option . . .

Sleepwell Cemetery, Los Angeles. The middle of the night, give or take a few minutes. It wasn't tactful to go about digging up bodies during daylight hours, what with grieving relatives placing fresh flowers on the plot next door. This was business that needed the dark, and they'd got it, the spotlight trained on the grave excepted.

Lori stood by in a long black leather coat while three Deveraux employees went to work with their spades. Authorisation for the exhumation had come through that morning from Spy High, and Mr Deveraux had thought it more cost-effective to use their own men for the entire procedure. It would save the expense of mind-wiping the cemetery's legitimate employees afterwards. Lori hadn't realised that computer brains could be so thrifty, but she felt better with Deveraux men here. And Shades. Watching the grave open up like a wound in the earth was not what she called a fun evening.

'Makes a change from *Metro*, doesn't it Lori?' said Shades Carmody, gently critical.

'Makes a change from Spy High,' Lori grunted. Was her mentor telepathic or what? 'I feel like I'm auditioning for a part in that old Buffy The Vampire Slayer show from Twentieth Century Gold.'

'I don't think we need to worry about vampires,' Shades said.

They'd soon find out. Instead of soil, spades were striking against the mahogany of Dane Stockdale's coffin. Time to bring it up. The crane moved into position.

This is not pleasant, Lori shuddered, wrapping her coat more tightly around her. This is really not pleasant.

The coffin was lifted like buried treasure. It swung a little in the air, suspended from the crane. The spotlight caught it and Lori saw it was carved from the same wood as Susan Stockdale's sideboard, though in slightly less polished condition. Three years in the ground didn't do anything any good.

What would it have done to the body *inside* the box?

The coffin was lowered to earth, loosened from the crane. It had a lock and a catch in rusted brass. The Deveraux men gathered round, clearing clods of dirt with gloved hands. Lori *didn't* want to gather round. She didn't want to be anywhere near here. The lights of the living Los Angeles seemed very far away.

They broke the lock. Susan Stockdale didn't have to know.

They raised the coffin lid. It groaned like the door of a haunted house.

The Deveraux men peeked inside. Their faces, part white, part shadowed, were not horrified or disgusted as Lori knew hers would be, but puzzled, almost intrigued.

'Agent Blue, Ms Carmody,' one of them called, 'you'd better look at this.'

'Is it *empty*?' Lori asked, hoping that were true.

It wasn't.

Her training took control of her legs and forced them to move. Shades was reassuringly close. They reached the raised coffin lid. Lori peered over it as she might have done over the edge of a cliff.

Dane Stockdale was in residence all right, but something was wrong.

He was perfect. The suit in which he'd been buried, the plush satin lining of the coffin on which he'd been placed, they were beginning to rot, but the dead man himself looked like he'd just stepped out of the shower.

'I don't believe it,' Lori heard someone mutter. 'Three years in there and not a sign of decay?'

Death is but a sleep, a priest had once told her, a sleep from which one day all will wake.

Lori heard herself scream.

Suddenly, without warning, Dane Stockdale opened his eyes.

THREE

His right arm lashed out, moving with a speed and strength not normally associated with limbs belonging to dead men. His right hand clamped like a vice around the nearest Deveraux man's throat. It squeezed. The unfortunate victim, eyes bulging, mouth gaping, struggled to prise the fingers from his windpipe. Couldn't do it. They were like bands of steel.

'He's alive! He's *alive*!'

'Help Peters! Get those fingers *off* him!'

The strangled man's companions wrestled with Stockdale's arm as well, and with similarly minimal effect.

'Luanne,' Lori breathed. 'We've got to do something.' If only she'd brought with her a weapon of some kind, a shock blaster, her sleepshot, but who'd have thought it necessary to go armed to an exhumation?

'Get out of the way!' Shades Carmody was shouting to the men. 'Out of the way!'

But Stockdale's left hand was active now, clenched around a second throat, and all the while he lay on his back in his coffin and said nothing – what do you say after three years in the grave? – with his eyes open and expressionless and glittering like glass. It was an awkward position from which to keep two men helpless and to resist the bludgeoning blows of a third.

So Dane Stockdale sat up.

He cracked the heads of the men he held together with skull-shattering force and the sound, like clay pots bursting, sickened Lori to her stomach.

But it also gave her courage. As the thing in Stockdale's coffin flung the Deveraux men aside, stood up, stepped unwaveringly on to solid earth, fear of powers occult or supernatural vanished. This wasn't a dead man returned to life. Zombies did not exist. There had to be another explanation, a rational one. And as a graduate of Spy High it was her duty to find it.

Even as Stockdale was hoisting the third and final man into the air, slamming him down into the coffin whence he'd come, Lori was shrugging off her coat and launching into an attack. Nothing to shoot him with? Fine. Fists and feet would have to do. She opened with a kick to the chest that would have floored a redwood.

'Lori, no!' Shades was discouraging.

Dane Stockdale wasn't even staggered. But he was alerted to a new opponent. Lori tried again, her kick ramming up under Stockdale's chin. Any normal man's head should have snapped back, dislocating the vertebrae in the neck and putting him in traction for a month. Stockdale's head juddered a little as it absorbed the impact, but that was all.

Okay. So she wasn't fighting a normal man. She'd pretty much worked that out already.

'Lori, leave him to me!'

And she might have abided by her field handler's instruction had Dane Stockdale at that moment not lunged forward and seized a third warm, tender throat in as many minutes.

Lori gagged, thrashed from side to side, kicked out at her assailant desperately. The cold, inhuman fingers tightening; they'd tear through her flesh like paper. If she remained conscious long enough, she'd see her larynx plucked and bleeding in his hand. She kicked lower, at parts of the body customarily avoided, even in combat situations. It made no difference. Dane Stockdale was not sensitive there.

Shades's voice was booming in Lori's brain as through a badly distorted sound system. Her sight was fuzzing too, like that of someone with weak vision who'd forgotten their spectacles. Her mind, starved of oxygen, drifted.

She vaguely registered Shades removing her glasses, could just about make that out as she writhed from Stockdale's extended right arm. And she thought her handler's left eye seemed unnaturally bright, twinkling like the little star in the nursery rhyme.

Only, in the nursery rhyme, the little star didn't suddenly let fly a laser bolt.

It flashed only inches away from Lori's face. And it almost caused a reaction from Dane Stockdale, his formerly impassive brow wrinkling slightly in confusion. Still no voice, though, no crying out, which would have been the likeliest human response to having your right arm severed just above the wrist.

Lori fell to the ground. She tore the now gripless hand

from her throat, saw the cable veins and steel bones dangling and prodding from the scorched and artificial flesh. No wonder Dane Stockdale had worn so well six feet under. He was an animate.

And he was ignoring Lori now, advancing instead upon Luanne Carmody. Shades was standing her ground. Lori saw her eyes in sharper focus now, and for the first time. The implants, they were beyond the usual black and multi-faceted insect eyes that most patients in need of a sight supplement had fitted. They seemed to flicker like computer screens. They seemed to calculate.

And the laser capability of the left eye was not in general public usage.

Shades's second bolt pierced the animate's chest through what for humans would have been the heart. For artificial constructs such as the disinterred Dane Stockdale, it was the central motor control. The laser ran him through like a javelin and speared him to the grass. He dropped to his knees, his arms by his sides. The third bolt entered the forehead just above the eyes and exited the back of the skull just above the spinal cord, having fried the animate's computer brain in the meantime.

There was no need for a fourth.

'Lori, are you all right?' Shades helped her up.

'I'm fine. Really. Thanks to you.' Lori felt it was a bit like gawping at the disabled but she couldn't help herself. Up this close she could see every detail of her field handler's lidless and unblinking optical implants, the figures and the symbols that flashed across the right eye, the radar screen that seemed to have been miniaturised to embellish the left. 'I had no idea . . .'

'The product of Deveraux physical re-engineering,

opticals division,' Shades said. 'State of the art, as you'd expect. If I was killed while on active duty, my eyes would be able to continue to transmit visual data back to Spy High for at least three hours.'

Lori winced as though she didn't quite like the sound of that.

Shades smiled thinly. 'My original eyes weren't anywhere near as useful. You know the old saying, every cloud has a silver lining? Mr Deveraux is very good at turning what might seem a setback to the organisation's advantage.'

'What about here, tonight? Three fatalities.' Lori didn't need to feel for pulses to know that the Deveraux men were dead. Apart from herself and Shades, only the crane operator had survived the evening: he was still cowering by his rig.

'Casualties now,' Shades acknowledged sorrowfully, 'but they've increased our chances of saving lives later, perhaps of saving the president's life.'

'You think this is linked to Simon's investigation?'

'We were led here thanks to Simon's anomaly file,' Shades reminded her student, 'and we've found a machine in a man's grave. So yes, I think so. Certainly, someone went to a lot of trouble to replace the human Dane Stockdale. They must have had good reason. Animates with this model's sophisticated self-defence and combat capabilities don't come cheap.'

'Almost as if whoever's behind this *expected* the body to be exhumed, so they left behind a nasty surprise,' pondered Lori. 'Someone expected suspicions over Stockdale's death sooner or later.'

'"Death" might be putting it a little strongly, Lori,' said

Shades. Her computer eyes examined the deactivated animate with analytical intensity. 'Disappearance might be more accurate.'

'I guess you're right,' agreed Lori. 'Because if he's not and never has been in his coffin, what is the real Dane Stockdale up to?'

'I had that dream again last night, Debbie.'

'Which dream is that, Mr President?'

'The one where I'm small and everyone else is big,' said Graveney Westwood, swaying from side to side in his chair like it was on the deck of a yacht rather than tucked neatly behind the desk in his temporary Los Angeles office. 'The one where I'm teensy tiny and scurrying about on the floor trying to avoid those big ol' shoes stamping down on me and squishing me flat like a bug. The one where no one can see me.'

'Ah,' Debbie Hunter nodded sagely, making notes. '*That* one.'

'You've got to put my mind at ease, Debbie,' the president implored. He lowered his head to the desk and covered it with his hands as if expecting those giant shoes to descend upon him at any minute. 'You've got to tell me again what it all *means*.'

'Oh, it's a good dream, Mr President, trust me,' diagnosed Debbie. 'It means you're in a privileged position. It means you can see things differently to anyone else. You have a new and unique perspective on events. Perhaps that's why the people trust you to be President.'

'You think so?' Westwood peeped from between his fingers like a frightened child from beneath the bedclothes. 'But if I'm President, I want to be *bigger* than everyone else to show them how important I am.'

'Ah, but being smaller demonstrates your humility, Mr President, sir,' interpreted the therapist. 'It shows how power hasn't gone to your head.'

'You know what, Debbie?' Westwood brightened, sitting up again and straightening his tie. 'I think you might be right. Humility. Yes, sir. That's what I've got. Humility. But just explain one more thing again for me about this dream.'

'Of course, Mr President,' said Debbie.

'How come I'm always *nekkid*?'

Debbie Hunter never got the chance to answer that particular question as just then somebody knocked at the door, an interruption for which she was no doubt eternally grateful.

'Who is it?' snapped the president. 'I told you I was with Ms Hunter and didn't want to be — oh. Gayle.'

And not alone. Accompanying the vice-president was a middle-aged black woman with dark glasses and a blonde teenager whom he thought he almost recognised. *Disturbingly* almost.

'Sorry to intrude on your important meeting, Mr President,' said Gayle Steinwitz with seamless irony, 'but I really feel you need to hear this.'

'Hear what? Who are these . . .' Squinting more closely at Lori. 'Don't I already know you?'

'We have met before, Mr President,' said Lori. Three years ago. Aboard the Guardian Star space station along with the rest of her team. While the president had been a crazed imbecile under the control of Dr Averill Frankenstein. At least the latter part was no longer true.

'I knew it. I knew it. I never forget a pretty face. Were you one of the Westwood Winners cheerleading team?'

'Not quite, sir,' said Lori. Immediately after the Frankenstein episode, Westwood had been advised to undergo a voluntary course of memory repression therapy, a milder version of a mind-wipe. It was either that or have the most powerful country in the world run by a gibbering, paranoid wreck. It seemed the therapy was still working.

'This is Agent Carmody and Agent Angel,' introduced Gayle Steinwitz. 'They work for the security services, Mr President. At the *secret* end. So before they start, perhaps it would be better if Ms Hunter found some work to do elsewhere?'

'Of course, Ms Vice-President,' said Debbie sweetly.

'Oh, no. Oh, no,' Westwood refused. 'You stay right there, Debbie. If this is any kind of bad news I may need you to put my mind at ease. Gayle won't mind you staying, will you, Gayle?'

'Of course not, Mr President.' Iceberg cool. 'If that's what you prefer. Agents Carmody, Angel, you'd better brief the president exactly as you briefed me.'

Lori let Shades do most of the talking. It was partly because her field handler was her senior anyway, partly because she didn't want to attract Westwood's attention more than was necessary. He was already glancing at her strangely, searchingly, as if his memory of their previous encounter was like a word he couldn't recall but that was on the tip of his tongue. Maybe it hadn't been a good idea for her to come after all. Shades had thought it would broaden her experience.

'What's that? What?' Luckily the reason for their

audience proved swiftly sufficient to engage the president's mind. There wasn't a lot of it to go round. 'So you think I *am* in danger here, and you think members of my own security services could be involved? Is this what you're telling me?'

'It's possible, sir,' admitted Shades. 'We would certainly advise you to proceed on that basis while we undertake further investigations.'

'You hear that, Gayle?' Westwood demanded. 'Was I right to let you carry out my engagements, or was I *right*? This great nation of ours could have been mourning its president by now. Well, t'hell with California. We can finance EPI by raising taxes. I want to be back at Camp Lincoln by this time tomorrow, d'y'hear what I'm saying? We'll stay there until this assassination scare is over.'

Camp Lincoln, Lori mused. The presidential retreat the public at large *didn't* know about – the genuine one. Camp David hadn't been used by American presidents for fifty years now. If terrorists ever attacked it, they'd only be assassinating animates.

'I took the liberty of anticipating your likely response to the agents' intelligence, sir,' Gayle Steinwitz was revealing. 'Instructions to prepare for departure to Camp Lincoln have already been given.'

'Peachy, Gayle, that's real peachy,' Westwood approved. 'Keep ahead of the game like that and you could be president yourself one day.' No response. 'Now can you show these fine people out while Ms Hunter and I resume our business . . .' He called after Shades and Lori. 'I appreciate the fine work you're doing in the service of this country. The people appreciate it . . .' The door closed behind them and Westwood's spirits sagged. 'That girl, if I could only place her . . . and did you hear that, Debbie? Someone wants to kill me.' He began to sway in his chair once more. 'Someone out there's planning to kill me.'

'Try not to worry, Mr President, sir,' Debbie Hunter counselled. 'You're among friends here. Vice-President Steinwitz. Myself. I won't let anything happen to you, Mr President. I'll look after you.' She wrinkled her snub nose.

'Will you, Debbie?' sighed the most powerful man in the world.

While back in her own office, 'But you've no *clear* leads yet?' Gayle Steinwitz was establishing not for the first time from Shades and Lori. 'Apart from this TAG operative Dane Stockdale, no suspects, no names?'

'That is correct, ma'am,' said Shades. 'But there's a nationwide APB out for Stockdale. His image has been programmed into our satellite surveillance system. If he reappears, even in Sacramento, we'll find him. The forensic report on the animate is also pending—'

'I'm sure it is. I'm sure it is. I'm sure you'll do whatever it takes.' Gayle Steinwitz leaned forward confidentially. 'I want to be kept up to speed on this investigation, Agent Carmody. Immediately. Directly. Do you understand me?' Agent Carmody did. 'Good. Very good.'

And Lori was drawn to the vice-president's eyes. Twin chips of blue. Cold. Clear. Like ice.

Even the students at the Carmody Dance Studio knew that the mirror walls in the studios could display more than reflections. Lessons could be enlivened and dance steps illustrated by a panoply of greats appearing for the purpose: Nureyev, Dame Margot Fonteyn, John Travolta. But they didn't know that the screens into which the glass converted also provided a link to a certain set of people who were far from household names, which was just how they liked it: Jonathan Deveraux and the techs at Spy High.

'So what have you discovered about Stockdale's animate, Mr Ferns?' asked Shades Carmody. She and Lori were eager to hear.

'Well, to start with, it's a fine piece of work,' admired the man with the white coat and the unfortunate head. It moved about a lot on his shoulders, as if attached to them by a coil of wire and little else. 'A most efficient model indeed.'

'It killed three people and wasn't far from making me number four,' Lori reminded the tech hotly. 'That kind of efficiency playing for the bad guys we can do without.'

'Of course, Agent Angel,' acknowledged the tech, head wobbling. 'I didn't mean to ... I was speaking purely from a technical perspective.'

'Perhaps you'd better continue, then,' suggested Shades.

'Of course. Well, essentially the animate was powered by a magnetic core that, barring accidents or, ah, laser rays, Agent Carmody, would have enabled it to function for ten years, perhaps longer if kept in the dormant condition in which you first found it.'

'It didn't stay dormant for long, Ferns,' said Lori.

'No, Agent Angel. Its internal systems included a solar activation mechanism. As soon as the animate was exposed to light after its original interment – when the coffin lid was opened – the mechanism was programmed to activate and fully re-energise the body. In effect, ladies, you woke it up.' Ferns grinned as if he'd made a joke.

'Did you find anything we can use?' Shades pressed.

'Before *you* put *us* to sleep,' muttered Lori.

'Sadly,' the tech lamented, 'the machine's systems went into terminal self-corruption mode as soon as its master program was disabled. Very little left for us to work with. However, if the manufacturer wanted to retain total anonymity, he missed a trick.'

'Keep us waiting very much longer, Mr Ferns,' said Shades, 'and there'll be a new president in the oval office before we've had a chance to save the old one.'

'Of course. Well, our analysis of the computerised and mechanical parts of the animate yielded nothing, but once we'd stripped off the epidermis and examined *that* . . .'

Epidermis? Lori winced. Skin.

'. . . well, *then* we discovered a microscopic serial number, the first part of which proved to be the registered trading code of an animate manufacturing company based not far from you, coincidentally. Las Vegas, Nevada.'

'And that is where you must go, Angel Blue.' The image of Jonathan Deveraux appeared on the screens alongside the tech. 'Immediately. Your flight and accommodation at the Olympus casino-hotel have already been booked.'

'Yes, sir,' said Lori, struggling to look serious rather than excited. On her way again. And to Vegas! The playground of the western world. A welcome change from digging up bodies in the middle of the night.

'You will investigate this company, this Action Animates,' Deveraux instructed. 'You will determine whether it is genuinely linked either to the disappearance of Dane Stockdale or to any plot to assassinate President Graveney Westwood. You have permission to pursue whatever leads you might uncover. Your field handler may accompany you to provide support services or you may venture into the field alone. That is your decision. All relevant information is being downloaded into your belt-brain. Good luck, Angel Blue.'

'Yes, sir. Thank you, sir.' Vegas. The original twenty-four-seven city. Glitter. Glamour. Gambling.

The walls of the dance studio had become simple mirrors again.

'Well, Lori?' asked Shades. 'Do I pack or do I stay here and make excuses to the students for why your lessons are cancelled?'

Lori thought back over the last six months. The surfing and the slacking. The parties and the boys. The reputation she seemed to have earned but didn't want. It all made her decision very easy. 'Luanne, I think this is something I need to do by myself. You were right, what you said the other day. I have had things on my mind. I have let my training slip. But this is my chance to maybe get things back to the way they were, to find myself again. The real Lori Angel.' She shrugged. 'Whoever that is.'

'Whoever she is,' said Shades warmly, 'I think she's going to impress us. You know where I am if you need back-up.'

'Yeah. Thanks.' Lori smiled. 'First sight of a rampaging animate and I'll come running. Oh, and Luanne . . .'

'Yes, Lori?'

'One last thing before I go. We couldn't just have a quick extra session with the *shuriken*, could we?'

In Las Vegas, Nevada, there are more than five million videphones. On one of them, a woman is calling a man.

'So much for secrecy,' the man says, amused, 'though I have to say you look well. The job obviously suits you.'

'This is not the time for idle banter,' the woman responds coldly. 'We may have a problem and it may be coming your way.'

'A problem? How stimulating. Describe it.'

The woman does. The man's amusement is undiminished.

'Is that the best they can do?' he scoffs. 'This woefully weak administration deserves to suffer, and I will see that it does. As for these "agents" you speak of, they will be provided for, I think the blonde girl in particular. This may or may not be her *first* visit to Las Vegas, but it will certainly be her *last*.'

FOUR

DEVERAUX FILE: From *The Secret Agent's Guide to the World* by E. J. Grant
UNITED STATES: LAS VEGAS, NEVADA.

From its earliest days, Las Vegas has been associated with crime. The first casinos were constructed in the 1940s, with the notorious gangster Benjamin 'Bugsy' Siegel making his mark on the history of the city in 1946 when he built the original Flamingo Hotel. Bugsy himself was shot dead six months after the hotel opened, but the Mob continued to be closely involved with the running of the Vegas Casinos for the next thirty years. This was perhaps not too surprising in a place that quickly became known as the gambling capital of the world.

Organised crime in the twentieth century sense is unlikely, however, to trouble the Deveraux operative of the mid-twenty-first. The Mafia, the Syndicate, the Mob, these groups were successfully purged decades ago. An agent assigned on mission to Vegas can expect to be faced by dangers of a more technologically advanced nature.

The city as it is now can trace its origins back to the late twentieth century and the rise of the themed mega-hotels and casinos flanking Las Vegas Boulevard or The Strip, the highway that cuts through the heart of town. Dazzling recreations of other times and places such as Caesar's Palace, New York, New York, the Luxor and the Venetian ushered in a golden age for Las Vegas. These casino-hotels were resorts in their own right. Employing cutting-edge technology and boundless imagination they provided an unparalleled and unique vacation experience for all the family, transforming Sin City from gambling mecca to an entertainment paradise for all ages.

This process has continued into the twenty-first century, with a new generation of extraordinary casino-hotels and an ever-increasing wealth of leisure activities. Central to Las Vegas's success now is the animate industry. Indeed, eight of the ten largest and most profitable manufacturers of animates in the country are located in the greater Las Vegas area. These companies provide mobile and interactive mythological creatures for the Olympus, the Valhalla and the New Luxor casino-hotels, historical figures for the American Way, and a variety of alien types for the Final Frontier.

They are also likely to provide a Deveraux agent with his or her reason to visit Southern Nevada on business.

The potential of animate crime poses a challenge not only to our own organisation but to all law enforcement agencies. Artificial constructs that have no fear, that feel no pain, that obey their programming without question or qualm, and that can be moulded to look like anything or anybody – in the wrong hands their capacity to create terror and destruction cannot be underestimated. At the moment a rigid and closely monitored set of regulations governs the industry, but what of rogue manufacturers? What if, beneath the smiling faces of the Las Vegas animates industry, something more sinister lies hidden?

To call it impressive was an understatement. Like describing the 'Mona Lisa' as a nice picture or Everest as a big mountain in the Himalayas. Inadequate. Lori groped in her vocabulary for superlatives – stupendous, maybe, or phenomenal, staggering, jaw-dropping, words like that – but she was a secret agent, not a novelist. And besides, sometimes an unsyllabled gasp could be just as eloquent.

The Olympus casino-hotel towered before her, *above* her. Olympus as in the home of the Greek gods, and though the name wasn't intended literally, if Zeus, Aphrodite and Co ever decided to take a quick vacation earthside, they could do worse than check in here. The lower levels of the hotel seemed sculpted from rock, like sheer cliffsides that had hammered their way out of the desert in search of the sky, but they were made from marble, marble stained green and pink and blue, and they were studded with windows, each one framed by doric columns in the ancient Greek style and roofed by a pediment. As the building soared higher the mountain motif was abandoned and the whole structure became a temple, richly decorated with friezes from Greek legend and history. Then, standing sentinel at the summit, imposing, gigantic, the triumvirate of brother gods who ruled over life and death: mighty Zeus with the thunderbolt in his hand, Poseidon of the ocean bearing his trident, and cloaked Hades, lord of the Underworld.

'Just as well we haven't got those guys to worry about,' Lori muttered to herself.

'Hi! I'm Nadia. How are you today?' It was a nymph with green hair, wearing a simple chiton, the dress favoured by the women of ancient Greece, also green, and leather sandals. She was accompanied by a centaur.

'Hi,' said Lori. 'I'm fine.'

'Would you like to check in to our hotel today?' pursued the nymph with a smile as fixed as if carved from the same marble as the hotel itself.

'The bags are a bit of a giveaway, aren't they?' said Lori. The centaur was obviously an animate. She wondered if the nymph was too. 'I mean – yes, please.'

'Pericles will be happy to escort you to the front desk,' said the nymph, 'but don't forget to be outside again on the hour every hour between seven and midnight to witness Zeus: The Thunderbolt Experience, one of the many highlights at the one and only Olympus casino-hotel, where mortals can live like gods. Enjoy your stay.'

'With a spiel like that, how can I not?' Lori wondered.

'Please, my name is Pericles. May I take your suit-cases?' said the centaur.

The pillared lobby of the hotel was just as dramatic as its exterior. It was thronging with chattering, exuberant people, rubbing shoulders with Medusas and Minotaurs and the occasional cyclops. A fat woman with an extravagant hairdo was having her photograph taken with Pan. Several little children were patting Cerberus, the three-headed dog who seemed to be moonlighting from his job guarding the entrance to the Underworld. Lori checked in quickly – her room was ready for her. Twentieth floor. Overlooking the Aegean Pool and Water Complex. A porter dressed as if ready to defend the lobby from the Persians whisked her bags away. Lori wandered with bewilderment into the central atrium. Bat-winged harpies and flying horses in pure white circled among the shafts of golden light above her. There was the prow of the Argo, the bronze giant Talos, the wooden horse of Troy. There was so much to distract her.

Apart from the fact that a good secret agent should *never* allow herself to be distracted, it wasn't surprising that Angel Blue was not looking where she was going.

The boy's package fell to the floor. The floor was marble. The contents of the package evidently were not. There was the sound of glass breaking.

'I'm so sorry,' Lori blurted. 'That's my . . . I wasn't looking . . . I'm so *stupid*.'

The boy was crouching down feeling the package like a doctor examining a patient complaining of stomach pains. 'Oh, no. Oh, no. It's smashed. It's shattered. There's nothing for it . . .'

'I am *so* sorry . . .'

The boy looked up in agonised concern. 'We're going to have to call the vase paramedics.'

'Say what?'

'Before it's too late. You know the guys, forget the bandages and the oxygen, just pass the superglue.'

'Vase . . . paramedics?' Lori frowned.

'It's okay. I'm kidding. It's a vase. It's broken. It *was* a present for my Aunt Mildred's birthday. Now it's scrap. But don't buy a ticket for a guilt trip. I never liked her anyway.' He stood, the package under one arm. The other he offered to Lori with his hand on the end of it. 'My name's Robbie Royal by the way. My friends call me Cas.'

'Cas? As in Cas short for Robbie?' Lori took his hand and shook it bemusedly.

'Not too hard,' the boy recommended. 'You don't want to break my fingers as well. No, Cas short for Casino. Casino Royal. That's what my friends call me.'

'You must have some strange friends,' noted Lori.

'Nah, it's because I was born and raised in Vegas. The city's in my blood. Cut me open and I bleed neon. Could be worse. They could have called me Craps.'

'I expect one day they will,' said Lori, still baffled. 'But like I say, I'm sorry about the accident and I'll be happy to—'

'It's your first time in town, isn't it?' guessed Casino Royal swiftly. 'What did you say your name was again?'

'Actually, I didn't,' said Lori, 'but it's Lori, and surprisingly enough, my friends call me Lori too, and yes, this is my first visit to Las Vegas.'

'Thought so, Lori. I can tell these things. That's why

you were looking up, down, left, right, backwards, side-ways, every way except right in front of you. Surefire banker bet,' he rattled his broken package, 'tinkle, tinkle, tinkle. The house wins.'

'And as I said –' more firmly now, uncertain where this impromptu conversation was heading – 'I'm *still* sorry we bumped into each other and if you'd like me to pay for a replacement for Aunt Mildred's birthday present I'd be happy to—'

'Buy me a coffee.'

'Pardon me?'

'Forget the vase. I'm a magnanimous kind of guy. I forgive you. I'm also a cheapskate. It was almost worth-less. Buy me a coffee instead. And yourself. Go mad. Have a coffee with me. Here and now.'

'You're sure of yourself, aren't you?' Lori said, though with a smile she couldn't repress. 'What is this? Get in with the new girl in town while she's still got money in her pocket?'

'Absolutely,' grinned Cas. 'You've seen right through me. So what have you got to lose? Coffee. You and me. Go on. Roll the dice. Take a chance. This is Vegas, Lori. Live dangerously.'

'Living dangerously I know about,' grunted Lori, 'and having a drink in a public place with you, Mr Casino Royal, is not it. So yeah, why not? Coffee for two it is, though if you're after a meal as well, you can forget it.'

And he was good-looking in his way, not as classically handsome as Ben or as excitingly dangerous as Jake, but kind of easy-going on the eye. Hair what you might call off-black in colour and spiky without making a state-ment. Eyes brownish, and sparkling like they'd just been polished. Actually, *twinkling* might have been a better word, with amusement at some joke he had yet to share. His lips too, always parted in a smile. Casino Royal treated the world with high good humour, and expected to be treated the same way in return. It made him entertaining company.

Lori realised that she shouldn't keep comparing him to Ben and Jake, particularly as this was just a casual, accidental meeting and unlikely to lead to a sequel – sequels almost never lived up to the quality of the original – but she couldn't help it. Cas was clearly intelligent and witty, a class above the boys she'd been dating lately, but also free of intensity and the need to prove himself and to approach to each day as if it was a contest he had to win. His philosophy, if he really had one, seemed to be very simple: 'The way I see it, life's a gamble, which is why Vegas is such a cool place to be. All of life is here. Everybody playing the game. The way I see it, you roll the dice and you take a chance.'

'So what do you do when you're not rolling dice or colliding with tourists in the lobbies of hotels?' Lori probed. Cas was probably a couple of years older than her. Twenty, twenty-one, maybe. 'Are you a student or do you have a job?'

'No and not really,' Cas replied.

'What does not really mean?'

The boy grinned. 'It means a little bit of this, a little bit of that. *Lots* of that if I can get it. It means I live on my wits and my smile and my other assets.'

'So times are hard, then,' said Lori.

'Ouch. That one hurt. She smashes my vase then shatters my ego. So what about you, Lori? Are you a student or do you have a job?' She told him. 'Dance? So you could teach me some moves?'

'I said instructor, Cas. Not miracle worker.'

'I don't want any of that moon mood stuff everybody's doing. I like something with a bit more gravity.' Casino leaned forward enthusiastically. 'What about the tango? Do you do the tango? Or that dance that got banned in Brazil for being too *spicy*.'

'The lambada?'

'Yeah, the lambada.'

'Baby, I warm *up* with the lambada,' Lori grinned. 'But right now I think I'd better try and find my room.'

'Need any help? There are five thousand rooms in this hotel.'

'Luckily, they told me which one is mine in advance.'

'What about later?' Casino was indefatigable.

'What *about* later?' Though she guessed and it made her feel surprisingly good.

'Mr Robbie Royal at your service. Local tour guide extraordinaire. Small, select groups. One to one attention. Let me show you around. It's a big town. I promise to stop you falling over anyone else and destroying their shopping like you did mine.' He patted the forlorn package on the table between them by way of reminder.

'See you again, you mean?' Lori feigned careful deliberation. 'I don't know . . .'

'Go on,' Casino dared. 'Roll that dice. Take that chance.'

'You're not gonna give up, are you?' And it might be fun. Her appointment at Action Animates wasn't until tomorrow. 'Okay. What if we meet here, about seven?'

'Here and about seven works for me,' said Cas. 'One

thing before you go, though. You never did tell me the rest of your name. You know, in case I have to get the girl at the desk to call up or something.'

'Angel,' said Lori.

'Get out of town. So I'll see you later, Lori Angel.'

Oh, yes, Robbie 'Casino' Royal thought to himself as he watched her walk away, he'd see her later, all right. That old broken vase routine – it always worked.

For her date with Cas, Lori wore her suede boots and jeans, her strapless rainbow chiffon top and slung a denim jacket over her shoulder. She doubted he'd be disappointed.

He wasn't. 'Hey, what about we just kind of run into each other like we did before, only this time I'll be ready.' He opened his arms wide.

'Arm's *length*, buster,' warned Lori playfully.

'At least I've got an idea for tonight that matches the company.' He flourished a pair of golden tickets in front of her eyes.

'Don't tell me we're going to Willie Wonka's Chocolate Factory?'

'All right, I won't. But we're not. There's only one place in Vegas suitable for an angel. The Garden of Eden.'

'Come again?'

Cas explained during the cab ride along the multi-tiered lanes of the Strip. 'The Eden casino-hotel and entertainment complex is the latest mega-resort to open round here. Actually, it hasn't really opened yet. That's next week. But they say it's magnificent. Paradise Lost has been Regained. That's what they're saying. The centrepiece is a self-contained walk-through recreation of the Garden of Eden itself, complete with all kinds of tropical flowers, plants, a lot of wild animals you can touch and feed and stroke and all that kind of stuff, if you've got a thing about wild animals, that is. 'Cause they're not actually that wild. They're animates. Everything in Eden is artificial. I think they think it'll last longer that way.'

'And don't tell me,' said Lori. 'They do a great line in fig-leaf lingerie, and maybe a perfume called Original Sin, and the toilets say Adams and Eves rather than Men and Women.'

'You've been reading your guidebooks, Lori. I'm impressed.'

'No. Just guessing. But if it doesn't open until next week, Cas, how come we're heading there tonight?'

'Because of the special pre-Grand Opening party there tonight. VIPs only. A preview of paradise. Wolf Judson himself is going to be there.'

'I know I'm from out of town, but who?'

'Wolf Judson. Eden's owner. Actually, probably about half of Vegas's owner.'

Lori was suddenly reminded of the Gun Run back at Deveraux. 'Is he anything to do with the Judson arms manufacturing family?'

'He's all that's *left* of the Judson arms manufacturing family,' said Casino. 'A girl who knows her guns. Now I'm not only impressed but afraid.'

'Don't be stupid, Cas,' scolded Lori, 'though I can see that'll be difficult. Just tell me – and no disrespect intended – I hardly think you qualify as a VIP, not even in Vegas, so how'd you get the tickets?'

The cab drew to a halt and the door was smartly

opened from the outside. 'Saved by the bellboy,' grinned Cas.

Because as soon as they stepped inside the Eden the issue of the tickets vanished into irrelevance. All that mattered to Lori, Cas and their hundred or so fellow guests was the extraordinary panorama before them. It was as if the tropical forests and the wild places of the earth had been bred with alien jungles and cultivated here to provide startling scenery for twenty storeys of hotel rooms. Plants and flowers and trees in psychedelic colours, flora that no longer existed, that could never have existed, burgeoned and bloomed in twisting, turning shapes to form a landscape of strange, surreal beauty and harmony. And the beasts that Casino had promised – lions, tigers, elephants, bears, alligators and dodos, species extinct as well as extant – all teemed tamely together, Nature's great kaleidoscope under a vast dome of glasteel.

'Let me assure you, however,' said Wolf Judson once cocktails and canapés had been distributed, 'that the glasteel is not for security reasons. Not a single guest at the Eden casino-hotel is going to be able to sue for the loss of a limb to any of my animate pets.' Polite laughter from the assembly. Of course, as Lori well knew, every-thing that rich men said was received with polite laughter. 'I'm afraid, if any of you are considering staying here in order to quietly feed your husband or wife to the lions, you are going to be disappointed.' More polite laughter, perhaps a little strained from one or two quar-ters. 'The environment simply requires a strictly controlled temperature. Now, please, I have bored you long enough. Explore Eden at your leisure. Wander the unpolluted paths of paradise where only Adam and Eve have walked before you. But remember, beware of the Serpent.'

'Are we going in?' said Lori.

'Are you kidding?' said Cas. 'This is the only chance to enter Paradise I'm likely to get.'

Wolf Judson stood greeting his guests individually at the entrance. He was well-named, Lori thought as she and Casino queued to shake his hand. His silk suit couldn't disguise the strength and power of his body. His hair was thick and dark, though flecked with the same grey as his beard, and tied back in a ponytail.

And was she imagining it, or did he notice her while she was still a long way off and keep returning his glance to her periodically thereafter? He looked almost about to wolf-*whistle*, but when they were finally face to face the owner of the Eden contented himself with a compliment. 'Good evening, and may I say it's to meet charming young people such as yourself that I attend these otherwise tedious occasions.'

'Mr Judson.' Lori took the proffered hand. It gripped hers strongly.

'Please, my dear. Call me Wolf. And you are . . .?'

'Lori Angel.' He wasn't letting go.

'Really? A name as delightful as the person to whom it refers. And what brings you to Las Vegas, Lori Angel?'

'A holiday. Just a holiday.' She could throw him, of course. Though to upend one of the most influential men in Nevada in public was not perhaps the most advisable thing to do.

'You needn't sound so apologetic, Lori,' said Wolf Judson. 'Holidays are wonderful times, particularly here in Las Vegas. You never know who you'll meet or what's going to happen next.' His lips peeled back in a smile. The wolf baring his fangs. 'Enjoy your holiday, Lori. I'm afraid all too soon it will be over.'

And her hand was released.

Casino filed past Judson and wasn't even favoured with a word. 'What was that all about?' he said as he and Lori entered Eden. 'For a moment I thought old Wolf was gonna sweep you up in his arms and run away with you.'

'I don't think so,' Lori said without humour.

'Don't knock it. A family as rich as that — if he had a younger sister I'd be interested. Heck, if he had an older sister I'd be interested, a maiden aunt, so long as she had all her own teeth . . .'

'Cas, Casino, knock it off,' Lori snapped. Her hand was still smarting from Wolf's grip. The *arrogance* of the ultra-wealthy. 'I'm not rolling the dice and taking my chance with Wolf Judson, no way never. And watch out. You're about to step on a crocodile.'

Casino deftly avoided any inappropriate interactions with reptiles and the two of them wound their way through the lush, false vegetation towards the centre of the Eden environment. There stood the Tree of the Knowledge of Good and Evil. Its size reflected its importance in the Adam and Eve story, the trunk was metres thick and so high it scraped the glasteel roof, the branches many and strong and reaching out above the guests, laden with plump, ripe fruit that seemed to drip with tempting juice. A large number of people were gathered around the tree. The Serpent was due to appear.

'It's amazing,' observed Casino. 'It's all so real. The fruit looks good enough to eat.'

'I think you'd have problems if you did,' remarked Lori, 'and more from indigestion than Original Sin I'd say.'

'Imagine if you could still grow a tree like this,' fancied Casino. 'Whole orchards full of Trees of the Knowledge of Good and Evil. That'd be something.'

'Are you feeling all right?'

'Oh, sure. Are *you*, Lori? I mean, are you glad you took the chance and came with me tonight?'

'I can think of worse ways to spend an evening.' Waiting for death at the hands of a master criminal, for example, which was always an option for Deveraux graduates.

'Then what are the chances of you expressing your appreciation in the customary fashion?' Casino puckered up.

Lori rolled her eyes. She'd known it was coming. But why not? A bit of a kiss in the Garden of Eden didn't mean they'd have to get married or anything.

Half a minute later, it was obvious that Casino Royal was not a boy to squander his opportunities.

'Here it is! Look! The Serpent!' There was excitement among their surrounding invitees. Something was materialising, coiled around the trunk of the tree. Something scaly. 'What great special effects,' someone said.

'Cas, can we pause a second?' Lori eased herself out of his arms. 'Don't you think we should see this?'

'A big snake or you, Lori,' said Casino. 'I know who I'd sooner look at.'

But the Serpent was making an impact. As Lori watched, its sinuous body solidified, more like a dragon than a snake, scales gleaming, a flat reptilian head regarding its audience through cold yellow eyes. When it hissed and its forked tongue flickered, people flinched, even cried out, then laughed to cover their embarrassment.

'Would you eat the forbidden fruit on the advice of *this* guy?' Lori asked, turning to her companion. 'Casino? Cas?'

He was gone.

Normally it wasn't a problem for him. A simple, straightforward scam. Loiter in the lobbies of the major hotels until you spot an unaccompanied female checking in, young or old are best, less experienced on the one hand, more vulnerable on the other, all with more money than sense. Engineer an accidental collision and a broken gift for added guilt. Get them to have a drink with you. Use all that Casino charm. Roll the dice. Get their names. Get a date if possible but don't worry if not. Hack into the hotel's computer system either way to establish their room number. Employ those slick pick-pocketing skills to relieve them of their keys, during the date or in the street if they hadn't fully fallen for the twinkling eyes. Steal everything you can get your hands on.

No, normally it wasn't a problem, Casino thought as he paid the cabbie and rushed into the Olympus. He couldn't afford it to be. It was one of the many twilight ways he kept his life together. And why should tonight be any different?

Two words, as he turned her room key over and over between his fingers. Lori and Angel.

Why couldn't he just reduce her in his mind to the disposable status of gullible victim? She was rich enough to stay at the Olympus – she could afford to lose whatever she had in her room. And she was blonde and attractive – there'd be plenty of volunteers to dab her eyes with a tissue when she realised she'd been robbed.

He'd do it himself if that wasn't defeating the object.

He darted inside the elevator, headed for the twentieth floor.

But there was something about her. She wasn't like the others. He hadn't had to kiss her to lift the key from her jacket pocket, but he'd *wanted* to. He *liked* her. And he *didn't* like what he had to do to her now. It was just too late to stop.

Twentieth floor. Room 2045. Bizarre. The year he was born. What odds would you get on that?

Old Lennie had told him once that if you started getting twinges of conscience, that was the time to quit the game and join the unexciting law-abiding, because it was conscience that got you caught.

Casino wasn't denying it as he opened Lori's door. Maybe he should consider a new career or one day, maybe he'd end up paying. He stopped dead.

Why was the window open? The windows *didn't* open because that'd mess with the air-conditioning.

He reached for the manual light-switch but another hand was there first.

It was a big night for intruders in Room 2045.

FIVE

She'd felt him fumbling in her pocket, of course. Casino probably thought his sleight of hand was undetectable, but then he hadn't been trained in the art of espionage at Spy High. She could have confronted him then and there. In front of the Serpent, the tempter, in the Garden of Eden, it would have been fitting. But two reasons prevented her. One, what if Casino was more than just a street hustler, a chancer on the make? What if he was somehow connected to her mission? And two – well, two was that part of her simply didn't want to believe it. She'd hoped Casino was better than that.

Where were the nice, normal boys in the world?

She raced out of the elevator and towards her room. She couldn't have been far behind him. If she hadn't, rather unprofessionally, allowed her attention to be drawn to the snake in the tree, she'd have been able to keep the snake in the grass in sight the whole time. Chances were he was still in her room.

She tried the door. Shut but not locked. 'Okay, Mr

Casino Royal,' Lori announced as she pushed it open, 'your time is . . .'

A muffled shout of warning. Shadows looming from deeper darkness.

Lori was diving forward before she even saw the flash of the shock blasters. 'Lights on!' The room's comfort systems could be activated orally if the guest had taken the time to record a sample of his or her voice. Lori had. She landed on her hands, kept her legs together, and as if she was performing floor exercises in gymnastics, sprang herself up and over, making herself a missile.

A second of light for a Deveraux agent was enough. She'd taken in the two armed men, jet-packed, masked and in black spandex, one struggling to hold Casino.

She directed her boots at him.

They rammed into the man's chest and staggered him backwards. Casino tore himself free. 'Lori!'

She dropped to the floor with stunning speed and the shock blast flashed impotently above her. Another leap, lower this time, took the assailant's legs.

'Shoot her in the back, huh?' Casino brought a lamp down on the first man's head by way of deterrence. It was unlikely to be successfully activated either orally or manually again.

'Casino, get out of here!' The second man was standing again, behind her as she turned to Casino. She swung an elbow back into his stomach. 'This is nothing to do with you.'

'So sue me!' retorted Casino, searching around avidly for more free-standing furniture to smash. The desk chair looked promising.

But the intruders had had enough. They backed to the

window, energising their packs. Cas swung the chair but hit only the wall. Lori grappled with the second man but the boosting power of his jet pack was too much and he managed to shake her off.

Casino watched them fly out the way they'd evidently flown in. 'Friends of yours, Lori?'

Lori wasn't watching anyone. She was too busy flinging open one of her suitcases, reaching for a jet pack of her own.

'What's that doing in there?' Casino said, startled. 'Is that *yours*?' Lori fastened the jet pack over her shoulders with such dexterity that he was left in no doubt. And the metal bands that she clasped around her wrists, what were they about? 'What's going on?'

'Casino, I haven't got time for this. You've stumbled into something that's over your head. I suggest you stumble out again.'

The magnetic thruster that tapered down Lori's back glowed as the jet pack booted up with a tell-tale whoosh of imminent activity. Lori was standing at the gape of the window. Then she wasn't. Casino rushed to it himself and leaned out. He saw Lori, rising into the night sky.

He'd been right before. She wasn't like the others.

And she was thinking, Casino would need to be dealt with. He'd seen too much to be left alone. It was unfortunate but he'd need to be tracked down and mind-wiped. But that was for later, a *then*. Now she had a more immediate quarry to track down. Spandex-clad thugs with jet packs tended not to be routine criminals. Somehow, someone already knew of her presence in Las Vegas. She'd quite like to learn who.

The intruders were not such expert jet packers as

herself. They didn't know how to harness the air currents to assist speed and height. They were soaring up the side of the Olympus above her but she would catch them.

They saw her coming, shot wildly at her. Lori weaved through the shock blasts, controlled her direction with one hand and pumped out sleepshot with the other. Her enemies sought refuge among the titanic figures of the three brother gods. They took cover behind Hades. Evidently, as their aim improved, they were keen to send Lori to the Underworld.

And that was somewhere she had no desire to go. Lori increased her speed, both hands on her jet pack's control arms, looped around the peak of the hotel, rolled over in the air so that her back was to the ground. The thugs hung on to Hades's cloak to try to get a clearer shot. Made themselves easier targets. The jet pack buoying her up, Lori prepared to take them both out. Sleepshot primed . . .

To a tumultuous cheer from the distant ground, a sudden burst of lightning blazed from the rooftop. Lori was dazzled, blinded. Deafened by a booming and disembodied voice. 'Call me Zeus, the king of the gods, master of the thunderbolt and wielder of the lightning!'

Zeus: The Thunderbolt Experience was getting underway. Zeus himself seemed rather pleased by the fact. His towering form lit up and his animatronic head craned forward. Maybe he was wondering how mere mortals had miraculously seemed to gain the power of flight. If he was, it was a development of which he disapproved.

Another bolt of pyrotechnic energy only just missed

Lori. She felt her hair singe. The crowd below cheered all the more. Maybe they thought she was part of the show.

The two thugs saw their chance. While mighty Zeus was doing their job for them, while the blonde girl was still struggling to force sight back into her eyes, they fled, jetting out across the neon night of Las Vegas.

But Lori recovered quickly, powered into pursuit. They'd made a hopefully decisive error. In the open sky, Lori's greater jet-packing skills would really come into play.

The Strip beneath her flowed by like a river of colour, like melted gemstones, magical, entrancing if she'd been simply sight-seeing. Shafts of light in orange and gold and green sprung from hotel roofs, advids unscrolling in space to boast of the latest virtual roulette and mind-slots you didn't even need to use your hands to operate. Ignore them, Lori commanded herself. Focus on the targets, almost within sleepshot range again.

Be ready. Judge the distance. She had them. *Focus*.

A helicopter cut across her path. A tourist, flight-seeing helicopter. The pilot intent on pointing out to his passengers the landlocked attractions of Vegas was oblivious to the presence of a secret agent in the sky alongside him. Lori had to rear up, away from the shredding slice of the rotors. A little boy with headphones on, his face pressed wide-eyed against the window, saw her and mouthed 'wow'.

Lori felt like mouthing something a little stronger. The chopper passed. Her view cleared.

The thugs had vanished.

Lori scanned all around. No sign. Maybe they'd dropped to the ground, in which case they could be anywhere, lost among the tens of thousands of late night revellers. Maybe their mysterious employer had arranged a rendezvous point below. It didn't matter now. However many maybes she could think of, they all led to the same, frustrating conclusion.

She'd lost them.

Most of her was astonished to find Casino Royal still in her room when she re-entered it via the window. Part of her, though, the part that always believed in the best of people even when circumstances suggested otherwise, that part of her was glad.

He was lying full-length on her bed with his ankles crossed and his hands behind his head, watching the videvision. 'At last. Do you know how *bad* this movie is I've been watching?' He turned the set off with the remote. 'It was pay-per-view, by the way. I've billed it to your account if that's all right.'

'Why are you still here?' she said frostily.

'What happened to the Goon Twins? Did you get them? I'm betting those wristband things contain concealed weapons, right? You shot them out of the sky!'

'Why are you still here?'

'Come on, Lori, what else am I gonna do after what happened in here?' Casino swung his legs off the bed and stood up. 'Those guys were trying to kill you. You pack wings along with your swim-suit, though being you're an angel I guess I shouldn't be surprised. Do you think I could just walk out the door and forget about it all?' Lori unslung her jet pack. 'Here, let me help you with that.'

'I can manage, thank you,' she retorted defensively. The glad part of her? She had to repress that. She had to regard Casino as a temporary inconvenience, a possible threat to the integrity of Deveraux. 'What are you after, Cas? You think maybe a spot of blackmail might be more lucrative than ransacking my room? Think I might be in a position to pay you off to "forget it all"?'

'No, Lori,' Casino protested. 'Absolutely not.'

'Gamble on that and you'll lose.' Lori suddenly aimed her sleepshot at him. 'You were right about the wrist-bands, though. I could end it right here.'

'You don't want to shoot me, Lori. You're misunderstanding me. I don't want to take advantage of you. I want to help.'

'Is this the same caring Casino Royal who helped himself to my room key an hour or so ago and then proceeded not to take advantage of me by nipping up here to burgle my room? Or did I misunderstand your intentions then as well as now?'

'No. Cards on the table.' Casino avoided Lori's angry glare. 'I was scamming you. It's what I do. I'm sorry.'

'I'll bet you are. Took a chance on the wrong chick this time, Robbie, huh?'

'I don't reckon.' Casino smiled ruefully. 'But okay, let's try it another way. Let's see what cards *you've* got. Go ahead, Lori, if that's what you want. Shoot me. Put me out of my misery. I *dare* you.'

She knew she ought to. She could keep him here until the mind-wiping team came and that'd be Casino Royal out of her long blonde hair for good. As with Stephanie Lorenzo, Jake wouldn't have hesitated for a second. But then, Jake had never snogged Casino Royal. He wouldn't have bothered to look for the good in him.

Lori lowered her arm.

'Thank you,' said Cas, finding the courage to look at her directly again. 'I want to help you, Lori. We've both been playing games, haven't we? I'm not the person you thought I was but you're not exactly the person I thought you were either. You're no casual tourist. Who do you work for? The government?'

'It's not your concern, Cas.'

'But I want it to be. Those guys might have killed me, too. Like it or not, Lori, I'm involved. Come on, roll the dice. Give me a chance to do something better than pick people's pockets for a living. I could be your partner — junior partner, naturally. I've got contacts. I'm known on the street. Give me a chance to prove to you that I'm more than a thief.' And the slightly worrying thing was for Robbie 'Casino' Royal, he *meant* what he was saying. Honesty and conscience in the same evening. Old Lennie would have said his condition was terminal.

But it was what Lori said that mattered. She regarded him long and hard. He rather liked it. 'All right,' she finally decided. 'We'll do it your way. Maybe your local knowledge will be useful.'

'That's great, Lori.' He could have hugged her. 'So are you a teen agent or something? What do you want me to do?'

'Stop asking questions, for one thing,' she said, 'and you need to just go home for now.'

'What? How is me leaving you alone going to help?'

'I need to clear you with my superiors first, Cas,' Lori explained, 'find out precisely how much I can tell you, stuff like that.'

'Makes sense, I guess,' Casino pondered. 'You're not just trying to get rid of me, Lori?'

'If I wanted to get rid of you, I could have done it by now.' Lori patted her wristband. 'Go home, Casino. Here, use the desk pad and write your number down. I'll call you in the morning.'

'Yeah? Is that a promise?'

'Trust me.'

Casino grinned. 'I guess *one* of us ought to be trustworthy. But what if those guys come back?'

'They won't.'

'And what about the room? How are you going to explain no glass in the window and shock blast marks in the walls? The cleaner's gonna freak.'

'I'll put a really big "Do Not Disturb" sign on the door. This is Vegas anyway, isn't it? Weird things happen. Now *go*. I'll call you in the morning.'

'Okay, but Lori? I *am* sorry about earlier. It's been a hell of a first date, hasn't it?'

After he'd left, she sighed. After she'd checked the corridor to ensure he'd left, she sighed again. It had been difficult having to lie to him.

Shades answered the secure line instantly. Lori told her everything.

'You'd better move to the alternative safehouse right away,' the field handler advised. 'Otherwise, proceed with your appointment at Action Animates as planned. Only be careful, Lori. I'll initiate an investigation at this end to check whether our general security has been compromised.'

'Thanks,' Lori said, 'and Luanne,' cautiously, almost shyly, 'can you come out yourself? I think it might be wise for me to have support on the ground. Someone I know I can rely on.'

Shades smiled. 'I'll be there,' she promised. 'Now what about the mindwipe request? You need to provide the team with as many of the subject's details as you can.'

'Okay. He's male, caucasian, early twenties.' Lori sighed a third time. 'His name is Robbie Royal.'

Wilford Pettinger had a face like badly kneaded dough and a handshake like damp clay. Lori felt her own fingers sinking into it and covered her distaste with an official-looking smile. 'It's a pleasure to meet you, Mr Pettinger,' she said.

'Likewise, likewise,' the man replied. 'It's always a pleasure for Action Animates to welcome to its premises a member of the Animate Regulations Enforcement Board, even when the visits do come at such, ah, short notice?'

'Yes, I do apologise for that, Mr Pettinger,' said Junior Inspector Angel. 'I haven't been with the board long – only passed my final exams recently – and I think one or two of my inspection notifications are still late being sent out. But I can assure you, you have nothing to worry about. My visit is strictly routine. I'm sure Action Animates has nothing to hide.'

'Of course not, Junior Inspector Angel,' said Wilford Pettinger. 'Perhaps a brief tour of the facility, then, and afterwards some light refreshments back here in my office?'

'A brief tour sounds like a splendid idea,' approved Lori. The more familiar she was with the geography of the place, the easier it would be to find her way around later, when the managing director of Action Animates was not watching her every move.

The company's plant itself was built some thirty miles from Las Vegas in the Mojave desert towards Arizona. 'It was more economical for us to develop a site here rather than nearer the city,' Pettinger explained. 'We're only a modest concern, though we have plans for expansion.'

'I'm pleased to hear it,' said Lori. 'Business is good, then?'

'Indeed. The demand from casino-hotels such as the Eden for animates of ever more versatile capabilities is increasing all the time. And our product,' Pettinger said proudly, 'is more than comparable to any other manufacturer's. Let me show you.'

He led Lori through the rooms where the animates were built. Here nervous systems of cable and wire were spun together like silver thread. There cyber-brains glittered in glasteel cases, waiting to be granted power of thought by the genius of their creators. Here steel limbs were wrapped in fabricated flesh. There a thousand pairs of eyeballs lined the walls in individual indentations, wide with the prospect of sight. Here mock human stomachs rested on tables, split open and empty, ready to be packed with vital mechanical organs, like a mummification in reverse. There the army of animates stood, naked and genderless, the breath of life yet to touch them.

'Very impressive, Mr Pettinger,' acknowledged Junior Inspector Angel. 'And are all these models intended for the Vegas market?'

'All of them.'

'So you don't ship *any* of your product out of Nevada at all, not even to neighbouring states? Say, for example, California?'

'We have never done *any* business with buyers in California,' said Pettinger. 'Why do you ask?' His lips twitched in what purported to be a smile but which Lori's studies in Body Language Analysis identified as a symptom of nervous guilt.

'Oh, no reason,' she said blithely. 'Only I'm sure I saw a report on a colleague's desk the other day to that effect.'

'No. I'm afraid you must have been mistaken, Junior Inspector Angel.'

'I suppose I must have been.' Lori smiled sweetly. 'But obviously, all your models are fitted with the regulation behaviour moderators.'

'Of course. Would you like to check?' A stonier invitation could scarcely have been issued.

'Oh, I doubt that'll be necessary,' Lori said. 'Only I'm sure I saw a report the other day – on a colleague's desk – that an Action Animate had acted beyond the parameters of the AREB's code. I'm sure it was in California. Its role name was *Stack* something, I think. I don't know. *Stuck. Stock . . .*'

'Perhaps it might be sensible not to pay so much attention to reports on other people's desks,' Pettinger said, 'particularly if one wants to be sure of one's facts, *Junior* Inspector Angel.' The emphasis was both a criticism and warning, Lori realised that. 'Besides, let me remind you that an animate's original manufacturer cannot in law be held responsible for any alteration to or customisation of a model's officially registered specification. *If* a product of Action Animates *were* to become a danger to human beings, the culpability would certainly rest with its then owner, *not* with us. And now,' Pettinger's politeness strained, 'perhaps you have seen enough, Junior Inspector Angel?'

'Perhaps I have.' Lori held her innocent smile in place.

'And perhaps you don't have time for light refreshments in my office after all. Time *is* getting on. You must be so busy, new to the job and everything.'

Lori wondered whether she should bait Pettinger further by claiming that no, she had plenty of time and would so much enjoy a cup of hot tea and a flapjack, but fun though it might be, it wasn't necessary for her mission. She'd learned enough. She was more than content for Pettinger to show her the way out.

It wouldn't be long before she was making her way back in again.

SIX

She scarcely needed the chameleon suit. Security after dark at Action Animates was laughably primitive – a few old-style electronic locks, a clutch of geriatric spy cameras and a handful of guards who'd have been better employed working their excess weight off at the nearest gym. But Shades had insisted she wear the suit, nevertheless. Shades's philosophy when commencing a mission was not to take chances, *never* to take chances unless and until there was no choice. Wishing you'd done things another way after the event was usually the prerogative of dead agents, who had plenty of time for regret.

Lori ghosted across open ground beneath the desert sky and slipped into the buildings of Action Animates.

Luanne Carmody was in Vegas. She'd set up a support base in a cheap motel on the outskirts of town. This was the Deveraux organisation's alternative safehouse, the kind of place shunned by the great casino-hotels, outside the neon shine of noticeability, where the greasy proprietor, who always seemed to be licking his fingers clean of fried chicken, asked no questions of his guests.

Lori waited for a wheezing guard to pass her by. No need to waste a sleepshot shell on him, even though he looked like he could do with a rest. She circumvented the animate construction areas. What she wanted to see was located in Wilford Pettinger's office.

Shades had told her that no traceable lapse of security at Deveraux had been discovered. If the jet-packed intruders had targeted her specifically, knowing that she was an agent, then *how* they knew remained a mystery. Lori had frowned. Shades had also informed her that a mind-wiping team had duly been assigned to Robbie Royal. Lori had continued to frown.

But now she eased open the door to Pettinger's office as if it was composed of the most delicate crystal. Closed it behind her, a hush of a click.

His computer was on his desk.

Lori deactivated her suit and removed the hood. Its infra-red panels were not designed for scouring computer files. She bypassed the security codes on Pettinger's machine effortlessly. Action Animates' most secret information was at her mercy.

Pettinger was obviously a fastidious records-keeper. There were the files for the design specifications of every animate constructed by the company going back to its inception. And there was a red file, protected, crudely, by further defences. Lori quickly breached them.

Dane Stockdale's file was waiting on the other side. It wasn't alone.

There were a score of names and the animates belonging to them. Tab Allenby. Karl Kreuser. Milton Lashman. Oliver Pound. Lori didn't know who they were, but if their photos were any indication, then all were mean and military, just like Stockdale. The dates of the animates' manufacture were spread out unevenly over the past three years. Stockdale had been the first. And they'd all been ordered by the same buyer.

Wolf Judson.

Suddenly, the owner of the Eden's interest in her last night seemed sinister rather than sleazy.

Lori took the disk from her belt and slotted it into the computer. She always liked to bring Luanne a memento from these visits.

'Downloading another's files without permission is an offence against the law, Junior Inspector Angel,' observed Wilford Pettinger. 'I fear your job might be in jeopardy. Hands in the air. Quickly.' He stood in the doorway pointing a gun at her.

Stupid. *Stupid*. She'd allowed herself to become too engrossed by what she'd discovered, had taken her eye off the ball, *and* the door. But who'd have guessed that Pettinger could sneak around so stealthily? No wonder he looked so pleased with himself.

'Move even a muscle, even a little,' he cautioned, 'and I will shoot you.'

'Working late tonight, Mr Pettinger?' said Lori.

'It appears I am not alone in that. Quite how you got this far I don't know, but Mr Judson warned me to expect a further visit from you – a visit without an appointment.'

'Did he? That was very foresighted of him. What else did Mr Judson say?' Pettinger's finger was trembling on the trigger. She'd have one chance to make one move. She'd better choose the right one.

Pettinger began, 'Oh, he said . . .' But he didn't finish.

Instead he slumped to the floor. Robbie 'Casino' Royal
stood in the doorway behind him. He too was holding a
gun, but by the barrel. He'd brought the handle down on
the back of the older man's head.

'Who cares *what* he said.' Cas grinned. 'Hi, Lori, did
you miss me?'

'Casino, what the . . .?' She was up and yanking him
into the office. Life as a secret agent was just full of surprises. 'What are you doing here?'

'Well not to sound too immodest about it,' said Cas, 'I
think I was saving your life.'

'But how . . .?'

'How did I get in here? Oh, I followed you from Vegas
and then just bypassed the security myself. I know a few
things about breaking and entering. I even dressed for
the occasion, can you tell?' Casino was all in black. 'But
there's nothing in my wardrobe to match *your* rig. When
I just saw you vanish out there . . . What is it? Some kind
of invisibility suit?'

'Kind of.' Lori felt more on edge now than when
she'd been staring down the barrel of Pettinger's gun.
Escaping certain death she could deal with – she'd done
exams in it – but coping with an x-factor like the
sudden, incredible appearance of Casino, that was
something else. Concentrate on practicalities. That was
the trick. Do what was necessary first and go from
there.

'Let's get Pettinger's body in here,' she said. They
dragged the unconscious MD further into the office,
enabling them to close the door again. Lori indicated
Casino's gun. 'You know how to use that?'

'In theory,' he said. 'But if you want to know the truth,

Lori, it's a bit of a bluff. Like in poker. It's not actually loaded.'

'Take Pettinger's,' Lori said, 'but leave any shooting to me.'

'Sure thing,' Casino accepted. 'I reckon you're the expert.' He watched as Lori returned to the computer and retrieved her disk. 'What are you here for, anyway? What are those guys up to? Making an animate of the president or something? Course, no one'd be able to tell the difference . . .'

'Casino. Quieter,' urged Lori. And then it occurred to her. 'How — ?'

'Did I avoid those guys you sent after me?' He winked confidentially. 'I know a few things about keeping out of sight when it matters as well, even without one of your fancy suit-things. That's how come I tracked you from the Olympus to that crummy motel – your organisation got budget cuts to make or what? – as well as from there to here. By the way, those guys you put on to me –' for a moment, Casino's expression turned hurt, accusing – 'they weren't gonna kill me, were they?'

'Of course not,' dismissed Lori. 'We don't kill as a matter of course, Cas. We don't kill at all if we can avoid it.' She thought of Jake. 'We're the good guys.'

'So what *were* they going to do if they'd found me? Suggest a relocation package to Atlantic City?' Lori seemed reluctant to respond. 'I've rolled the dice big-time to be here with you tonight, Lori. And I still don't deserve the truth?'

'Sometimes,' Lori said, 'it's safer not to *know* the truth.' But she heard what Casino was saying. 'Which is why my colleagues were going to mind-wipe you, perform a safe, simple little procedure that would have allowed you to forget everything about last night – forget that you'd ever met me.'

'*Allowed* me to forget? But I don't *want* to forget you. Why would I be here if I did? I want to know who you really are, Lori, what you do. I said it last night and for once in my lame underachieving life, I meant it. I want to *help*.'

'This isn't the time or the place, Cas,' Lori decreed. 'We need to get out of here safely, *then* we'll talk.'

'Well unless the place has suddenly turned into Fort Knox in the last five minutes, I think we can guarantee—'

'Wait.'

The gravity in Lori's tone made Cas pause. 'What is it?'

'The ring Pettinger's wearing.' She crouched by his insensate form to show it to her companion. 'It's flashing.'

'Well if you like it, take it. Perk of the job, right?'

'It wasn't flashing when he was conscious.'

'So what do you mean? It's some sort of signal?'

'I mean getting *out* may not be quite as straightforward as getting *in*.'

The sudden clangour of the alarm rather underlined Lori's point.

'Could be a fire drill, couldn't it?' Casino hoped. 'They have fire drills in the middle of the night, don't . . . okay, I know – shut up and leave the shooting to you.'

Lori led the way out of the office. From one direction came shouts and the drumbeat of boots on concrete. 'I think we'd better go this way,' she said, pointing the other way.

'And quickly, yeah?' Casino was abruptly aware of gunfire cracking around him.

'Yeah. You first. Go!' Lori dared a backward glance as they hurtled down the corridor. The half dozen guards in pursuit seemed younger and fitter than those she'd seen earlier, as if Pettinger had deliberately kept his best men in reserve. He'd sprung a trap and she'd fallen into it. *Stupid*, she cursed herself again. *Amateur*. She snapped out her arm behind her. Sleepshot reduced the number of their enemies by a third. They weren't caught yet.

Ahead of them, a sharp turn to the right. Cover.

'I lied,' Lori said, bundling Casino round the corner, stopping. She inched out again and fired the way they'd come, arresting the guards' charge at least temporarily. 'I want *you* to do the shooting now, Cas, though forget Pettinger's gun. Grab the blaster from my shoulder holster. *Now* would be good.'

Casino did as he was told.

'It's set on stun. *Don't* change it. Just keep firing, keep them thinking it's not worth their while trying to rush us. You think you can manage?'

'Only all night.' Casino took over Lori's position, announced himself with a barrage of shock blasts. A guard was knocked backwards, struck square in the chest. 'Got one!' In his enthusiasm, Cas leaned a little too far into their pursuers' view. The concrete of the wall beside his head erupted as bullets slammed into it. He jerked back quickly. 'Guess I shouldn't show too much of myself, hey, Lori?' She'd taken a step away from him and was rolling her hood down over her face. 'Lori, what are you doing?'

'You're right, Cas,' she said, pressing a stud on her

belt. 'So I'm not going to let them see *any* of me.' The chameleon suit worked its magic. All of a sudden, Lori was no longer there.

'Now that's cool,' approved Casino.

'Keep them occupied,' came Lori's disembodied voice, and was that a phantomly reassuring hand squeezing his shoulder? 'At least until I get there.'

'What? But . . .' Cas was going to protest that even though Pettinger's men couldn't *see* her, a stray bullet from any of their weapons could still hit her. Invisibility didn't also mean intangibility.

Or did it?

Either way, maybe he should spare a few worries for himself. *He* was very much in the line of fire, and though he took out a second guard, the blast's impact spinning the man round like a top, his comrades were bolstered by the arrival of several reinforcements. They were gradually advancing along the corridor towards him. Wherever Lori was, she'd better . . .

And then he knew where she was.

The air blurred as sleepshot shells propelled themselves into visibility a fraction of a second before they burrowed into the flesh of the guards. Two survivors ran for it. Casino was going to fire, but what if he struck Lori by mistake? Then again, what if the escaping guards summoned further assistance? *Which way should he roll the dice?*

It didn't matter. Each guard suddenly flew up in the air, thrown backwards by an unseen force, and crashed into unconsciousness. Casino couldn't help but laugh aloud.

A slim female figure garbed entirely in black materialised in a corridor of fallen men. She ushered Casino towards her. 'Shall we?' invited Lori.

And if they'd had time Casino would have thrown his arms around her and kissed her again like he had in Eden and this time he wouldn't have even picked her pocket. Mind-wiping aside, he was going to remember tonight for a long time.

And Lori was feeling confident as her memory of the plant led them towards the nearest exit. The alarm still jangled stridently, indignantly even, as if outraged that the two intruders remained at large. Well, it could make all the noise it wanted to. The door was ahead. A lone guard in the way was encouraged to move aside by sleepshot between the eyes. Lori kind of hoped Cas was impressed by the accuracy of her marksmanship. When they got back to the motel, maybe they *could* find time to talk.

There was no point in trying something fancy with the lock now. Just burst through the door and they were pretty much home free.

Pretty much.

Hidden holes opened in the door-frame. Jets of white vapour squirted out at head-height. They were breathing it in before they could stop themselves.

'Lori!' Casino coughed alongside her.

And suddenly the motel seemed a very long way away.

Lori realised several things at once. That she was conscious again. That she was lying on a softer surface than the concrete corridor of Action Animates. That she was no longer wearing her chameleon suit or, with cool air tickling her skin, very much else.

She was also alive, and she very much intended to stay that way.

Lori forced her mind free of the dregs of the gas and opened her eyes. There was jungle above her, exotic and lush, in a range of colours not always associated with the earth's natural habitat. And a glasteel sky. Above even that, softened by the intervening barrier, a tower of hotel rooms. *Eden* hotel rooms.

Lori was thinking Wolf Judson before she even sat up.

She grimaced. Wolf had obviously been raiding the Adam and Eve swimwear range. She was clothed – just about – in a bikini emblazoned with a fig-leaf motif. Casino, who was groaning himself into consciousness beside her, wore trunks in the same design. Lori doubted that their new attire had been provided for swimming purposes.

Not too far away, an animate lion roared.

'Cas, are you all right?' Lori crouched on her haunches beside him.

'I'm not sure. Are we dead?'

'Not yet. Come on, get up. We're in the Eden.'

'What?' Casino lurched on to an elbow, looked around in befuddled confusion. 'What are we doing here? What are we . . . wearing?'

'They've made sure we've got nothing that can help us.' Lori frowned. 'We have to get going. I *really* don't want to wait around until Wolf Judson shows up and tells us what he's got planned.'

'Wolf Judson?' Casino climbed to his feet. 'You're not serious?'

'Totally. Now come on.' Lori moved purposefully. 'The exit's over here.'

'I'm afraid, young lady, the exits are locked.' A man's

voice echoed beneath the glasteel ceiling. 'What kind of host would I be if I permitted my guests to leave before the entertainment?'

'Judson,' scowled Lori.

'Mr Judson to such as you,' said the voice. 'Or sir, if you prefer.'

'I've got a few names I prefer,' yelled Casino.

'Be silent, you absurd nonentity,' commanded Wolf Judson. 'I had more than half a mind to dispose of you at the plant, but my friends persuaded me it might be more amusing to include you in the little diversion I've arranged for Ms Angel.'

'Diversion?' Casino queried.

'He means death trap,' Lori supplied. 'It's the psychology of the megalomaniac. They're never content to just shoot you. They always try to kill you on a scale in keeping with their ambitions. It boosts their self-esteem.' She raised her voice and directed it to the jungle at large. 'And you must be about as arrogant as they come, right? Any guy who feels the need to recreate the Garden of Eden must be suffering a severe god-complex. What was the problem? Mummy never let you suck your thumb when you were a wolf cub?'

'You needn't speak so loudly, Lori,' said Judson. 'I can both hear and see you perfectly well. And please, spare us the amateur psychology. Every man worthy of the name seeks to impose himself on his world in one way or another. I intend to be more successful than most in my endeavours, that is all.'

'How's that?' Lori coaxed. 'What's your little animate scheme with Dane Stockdale and his pals?'

'Ah, now I'm supposed to betray myself and delay

your death by telling you all about my master plan, am I not?' A sinister chuckle dropped from the sky like icy rain. 'I'm afraid you may have to rewrite your text-books, Lori. What I *will* explain is what is going to happen to you.'

'It's not going to be good, is it?' anticipated Casino. He was already pretty sure that the roaring lion was coming closer.

'It was such a useful coincidence, you attending our little soiree here the other night,' Judson continued. 'It means you are already familiar with the Eden environ-ment, with the nature of our animates.'

'What are we listening to him for?' demanded Casino, pulling at Lori's arm. 'Come on. You said it. Let's *go*.'

'It's too late for that, Cas,' Lori said darkly.

Casino didn't seem to think so. He made off down the path. Didn't get far. From the scarlet of the surrounding foliage, the lion emerged. It faced Casino Royal and growled, which seemed somehow more menacing than the roar. Cas backed away. 'Maybe you've got a point, Lori.'

'Unfortunately for you,' Wolf Judson was explaining, 'my technicians have made a slight alteration to the pro-gramming of my menagerie. Whereas before the beasts were docile pets, now they are savage predators, con-trolled by myself, naturally. And you, Ms Angel, you and your insignificant boyfriend, are their prey.'

'Insignificant?' protested Casino.

'Boyfriend?' questioned Lori.

'This is Las Vegas, of course, the gambling capital of the world. We like to wager on everything here. So I have one or two friends with me placing bets . . .'

'On our survival?' Lori said, as a second lion appeared

to block the path's other direction. She and Cas were back to back.

'Your survival?' Wolf Judson's good humour boomed among the treetops like thunder. 'Oh, young lady, there is no possibility of your survival. No. We're betting on how long you'll stay alive.'

The two lions padded towards Lori and Casino. They bared their fangs, loped into a run.

'Your time starts *now*.'

SEVEN

'Cas!' It was the only syllable she needed.
  'With you!'

They knew what they were up against now. As the lions sprang, Lori and Casino plunged into the jungle.

Its floor was matted, springy with grasses, thick with creepers. Lori bounded over them. If her bare feet tripped here, any of Wolf's friends who'd wagered on under a minute would be in the money. With her left hand she swiped away the hanging foliage; with her right hand she held on to Casino. He was slower through the undergrowth, less used to life and death pursuits. But with two in one night, he was getting the practice.

'It doesn't matter where you run,' Wolf Judson's voice chuckled from overhead. 'I can see you.'

So could the first lion. It snarled through the vegetation, an ochre streak, its feral yellow eyes tracking them with electronic discipline. It wasn't a living animal, Lori reminded herself. It was a machine. It was programmed. That had to help them somehow. And soon.

'Let go!' gasped Casino. 'Maybe we should split up. Improve your chances.'

'Oh, no.' The trunk of a giant tree loomed ahead of them. Broken branches littered the ground around its base. 'We stand or fall together, Cas, get used to it.' The branches were just as false as the rest of Eden. They'd be designed not to rot, so no doubt were made from some kind of plasteel alloy. 'And now's the time to stand.' Lori drew to a halt, turned in the direction of the advancing animate.

'What? Lori, are you mad?' Casino's chest heaved with the strain of his exertions.

'Let's hope not.' She selected a branch as straight and as long as she could find, a branch from which you could carve a javelin if you had the time and the inclination. So Judson had removed from them any possible weapon. A successful agent in the field learned to improvise.

'Lori, what do you think you're doing?' Casino pressed back against the tree.

She showed rather than told him, braced herself for the lion's attack. 'Here, kitty, kitty.'

It had been programmed to do what a lion did. To bunch its muscles. To coil. To leap.

Lori ducked forward, stabbed up with her branch and with all her strength. She was beneath the springing beast, its soft, exposed underbelly. The plasteel shard sank in, ripped lab-grown hide like old carpet, pierced the creature's mechanical guts and severed wires like arteries and punctured valves like organs. The animate's internal damage alarm system was the desperate howl of a dying lion. Motor systems disrupted, the construct thrashed on the ground and flailed wildly with its paws.

It was on its back. With a shout of defiance, Lori drove her makeshift spear deeper into its mechanical innards, twisted, tore.

The beast twitched and was still.

'Wow. Lori . . .' gaped Casino. And then, 'Look out!'

The lion's companion was bearing down on her. Not launching itself but instead protecting its belly and making no sound – concentrating on the kill. Lori wrenched the plasteel branch from the neutralised animate and swung it round to oppose the operational model. She imagined Judson in a control room elsewhere in the hotel furiously programming the creature with fresh combat instructions. She doubted they'd be a match for Spy High training.

She held her spear at shoulder-height, two-handed, jabbing it in front of her like a hunter from the Stone Age. It checked the lion's advance. The creature reared, slashed out with claws like daggers, testing Lori's commitment to her attack.

Human eyes locked with animate's. Who was going to strike most quickly, most ruthlessly?

The lion's paw lashed. Lori lunged.

The spear impaled the construct through the neck. In one side, out the other, like the bolts in the neck of Frankenstein's monster. Oil and coolant pumped from the wounds. The animate writhed in its deactivation-throes, its paw catching Lori, knocking her to the ground. But she would get up again. Like its paralysed companion, this second lion would not.

'Bad guys nil, good guys two. Feel like adding to the score, Cas?'

'Lo . . . ri . . .' Casino had problems of his own.

An anaconda. Doing what anacondas did.

The coils of the constrictor were bunched around Cas's torso like tyres, tightening all the time. His arms were pinned helplessly to his sides. His bones would soon be cracking like dead wood.

'Hold on, Cas! Hold on!' Should she retrieve her spear, try to prise the snake away from his body? No chance. She needed to do something immediate. Casino was losing consciousness.

The anaconda's head thrust viciously, malignantly at her, hissed for her to keep her distance. Lori made a grab for Casino. The snake, outraged, opened its jaws as wide as possible. And Lori shoved her hand into its mouth. Then her fist. Then her forearm. And she clenched what she could and yanked and pulled. There were wires like metal strings in her grip and she tore them out by the roots. The anaconda's hiss became the clicking and whirring of a disabled construct. Its grip on Casino sagged. Gasping, his skin tattooed with the marks of the creature's scales, Cas disentangled himself and slumped against the side of the tree. Reptilian jaws drooling with oil slid slackly down Lori's arm. She flung her handful of electronic intestines aside with as much disgust as if they'd been offal.

'Lori . . . thanks . . .' Casino smiled weakly.

'It's okay. Are you all right?' She touched his ribs tenderly. Casino yelped. 'Are you hurt?'

'No. Ticklish.' He winked. 'Give me a minute to catch my breath and I'll be fine.'

'I'm afraid a minute is all you have,' interrupted the voice of Wolf Judson. 'A minute while I muster my troops, so to speak. Your continued survival has already frustrated several of my friends and, I have to concede, mildly surprised me.'

'Why don't you face me one to one, Judson?' offered Lori scornfully. 'I'll show you surprises.'

'A most tempting invitation, my dear,' acknowledged Judson, 'but I fear you'll need to conserve your strength. Two lions and an anaconda is an impressive start, but let's see how you fare against a brace of tigers, a grizzly bear, and perhaps a rogue rhinoceros.'

Casino looked at her bleakly and Lori knew that their tormentor was right. They could defeat *some* of the animals of Eden, but not *all* of them, not one after another in a relentless assault of tooth and claw. If they were going to live to see natural light again, they needed some way to incapacitate all the animates at once.

She tried to see things from Wolf's perspective as he directed the specified creatures towards them from his vantage point beyond the dome. He could see them, watch their every move, so there had to be cameras around – for Eden's general security, if nothing else. Cameras. Delicate wiring . . .

Lori hit on an idea.

'Cas, we've got to find a camera.'

'Say again? I don't think I'm up to holiday snaps.'

Lori scanned their immediate surroundings. 'I'm not fooling. It's the only chance we've got. He's watching us via cameras. Look for them. They'll be disguised as part of the scenery. Quickly, before we have company. Look for anything that's not right.'

'This whole place is not right if you ask me,' Casino complained. 'If the original was anything like it, no wonder Adam and Eve did a . . . and what do you think *you're* looking at?' A tall, thick-stemmed yellow flower, something like a tulip on steroids, was swaying and leaning in the air towards him, following his progress. When Casino moved, it did too, like a botanical shadow. 'Lori, I think our luck's changing.'

'You've found one.' Lori hastened over, parted the petals. At the heart of the bloom was the lens of a powerful micro-camera. 'Or in Vegas speak, Cas, you just hit the jackpot.'

'It will do you no good, girl, Wolf crowed. 'I have cameras throughout the environment. You cannot elude my animates, destroy this one if you will.'

'Thanks,' said Lori. 'I will. Lights out, Judson.'

Lori took hold of the flower's stem with both hands and heaved, uprooting it like some kind of obsessive gardener with a weed. There was a fizzing, a popping, an electric crackle. The plant came away from the soil in a shower of sparks.

'So that's one in the eye for Judson,' said Casino, 'but how's it going to help us with the animates?'

'What are all animals afraid of, Cas?'

Casino didn't have to say it. Sparks from the ruptured camera were already smouldering in the abundant and dry vegetation. Electricity sizzled dangerously too from the gash in the thin topsoil that barely coated the Eden environment's maintenance systems beneath. Had Wolf Judson buried them more deeply, Lori thought, he'd have been burying herself and Casino too. Now, though, they had a chance.

But they'd have to work fast. The pounding of hooves and a deep, blood-curdling bellow indicated more animates closing in.

'Grab a branch or something, Casino,' urged Lori. 'We need to stoke a blaze.'

The sparks that had smouldered were now beginning to burn. Lori drove a plasteel branch into the Eden's electricals, each thrust increasing the damage. Fire took hold there, too.

Casino joined Lori, tried to persuade himself that those yellow eyes gleaming at him from the jungle could not possibly belong to a tiger. 'But Lori,' he ventured, 'don't animates behave according to their programming? They don't have natural instinct, do they? They won't know they're supposed to be afraid of fire.'

'The fire isn't for the animates,' she replied, watching smoke rise toward the glasteel roof. 'It's for the sprinklers.'

And as Judson's animates closed in, the sensors that measured the temperature inside the Eden environment with the finest precision detected a sharp and sudden rise in one particular location. That information was transmitted instantly to the safety systems. Which reacted with their traditional response to fire.

It was as if Genesis had unilaterally decided to move on from the Garden of Eden to the Flood.

Water gushed from conduits webbed into the glasteel ceiling, sprayed from nozzles concealed in trees, geysered from sprinklers sprouting from the ground like metal mushrooms – water enough to drown the Great Fire of London inside a minute. Eden's designers had taken no chances.

Then another safety measure that Lori had hoped for kicked into action. Once a danger to the guests was signalled inside Eden, all entertainment functions ceased in order to facilitate evacuation. The emergency exits sprung wide. The animate animals closed down.

A rhino, a grizzly and a pair of tigers – frozen in mid-charge.

Unlike Lori and Casino.

'Run,' advised Lori, setting an excellent example.

The pair hurtled through the jungle. Maybe Judson could bypass the safety system somehow, reset the trap, but it would certainly take him longer to reprogram the computers than it would for herself and Casino to make it out of Eden, Lori knew.

So did Wolf. His voice boomed above the cascade of water for a final time. 'Well, Ms Angel, it seems I should be impressed. I underestimated you. You are a resourceful opponent indeed, which will make my ultimate victory over you all the more satisfying.' Lori and Cas broke across open land. An exit was only a sprint away. 'It seems my friends and I are all losers tonight. But as every gambler knows, there is always tomorrow. We will meet again, Ms Angel.'

Lori didn't even give him the courtesy of a reply. She wasn't playing games. She and Casino raced into the main lobby area of the hotel, their feet slapping wetly on the tiled floor.

'Well if Judson expects me to stay in *this* hotel he's got another think coming,' announced Casino. 'You don't reckon they've left our clothes around anywhere, do you? Or maybe a towel.' The droplets of moisture on his skin were like goosebumps.

' 'Fraid not, Cas.' Lori swept her bedraggled hair out of her eyes, wrung it like a cloth and splattered the floor with water. 'Until we get back to base, this is it.'

'The fig-leaf look. Terrific.' Cas peered down at himself in dismay. 'I'm sure these shorts are shrinking.'

'Come on.' Lori padded across to the main entrance. 'I can deactivate a locking mechanism this crude manually. Then, unless you've got some money stashed about your person in places I don't want to know about, Cas, we're walking.'

'Walking?' Casino's dismay was quickly worsening into acute depression. 'Like this? Dressed like this? Through town? Where people can see us? I think I'd sooner take my chances with the tigers.'

'Don't worry about it, Casino,' grinned Lori, her fingers dextrously disengaging the lock. 'You never know, we might even start a trend.' With a bleep, the doors eased open. 'After you.'

'Thanks. Terrific, Lori. I had a reputation in this city.' But sullen though he seemed, Cas didn't linger. 'Ladies and gentlemen, Ms Angel and Mr Royal have left the building.'

It was still night, though dawn couldn't be too many hours away and it was never actually dark on the streets of Las Vegas. Casino only wished that tonight had been the exception to the rule, that there'd been a catastrophic city-wide power failure or something. Because the other truism about the streets of Las Vegas was proving to be an unending source of humiliation for him: they were never empty, either.

'Hey, nice outfit . . . It's okay, you must have won your bet by now . . . Hey, Tarzan, you forget your jungle? . . . Heard about losing your *shirt*, but this is ridiculous . . .' Everyone had a line. Dancers leaving clubs, gamblers leaving casinos. Cas began to wish he could leave town.

Lori strode on oblivious to the rather less mocking and rather more admiring attention *she* was earning. 'It was bad news for us that the Eden hadn't opened yet,' she said. 'A week from now and Judson wouldn't have been able to pull a stunt like that.'

'No,' Cas concurred grumpily. 'He'd have probably tried something worse.'

'Excuse me, excuse me.' Their path was blocked by a little old lady clutching a small plastic bucket of coins, evidently her winnings from an evening on the slots. 'Are you young people anything to do with the Eden hotel?'

'No,' said Lori.

'*Yes*,' said Cas. Emphatically.

'Yes?' Lori turned to him in puzzlement.

'Trust me on this,' Cas muttered. Then, with a corporate smile to the little old lady he announced, 'I'm Adam and this is Eve. We're just one of the many promotional activities and events taking place around town before the grand opening of the Eden next week.'

The old lady's eyes lit up. 'Hiram! Hiram! Get over here!'

'You can take our picture as a unique souvenir of your visit to Las Vegas for the nominal sum of one quarter.'

'Hiram! Hiram! Bring your camera!' She nudged Casino in his anaconda-bruised ribs. 'And sonny, great legs.'

'I think you've got a fan there,' grinned Lori after the photography.

'I don't know about that. I've got a quarter.' Casino flourished the coin in his hand as if it was made of gold.

'End my misery, Lori, please. Tell me there's someone you can call to come pick us up.'

Shades was there in fifteen minutes. Driving back, she kept her optical implants very much on the road.

The following morning Casino was introduced to Luanne Carmody more officially, more solemnly, and more clothedly (thanks to the garments he'd magically found in the wardrobe when he woke). He'd spent the rest of the night in another room at Lori's motel. A Deveraux technical support team had also arrived. The motel's greasy proprietor was beginning to lick his fingers with renewed relish.

'I think we'd better have a chat, Casino,' said Shades. 'Lori's already briefed me. About you. About how the two of you met. About what happened last night.'

Lori was the only other person present in the room and was also attired more modestly though, to Casino's mind, not any the less attractively. A bank of computers made a sharp contrast with the accommodation's original shabby furniture.

'Did she tell you . . . everything?' Cas wondered nervously. 'About me, I mean.'

'If you mean, did she tell me that you're a two-bit con artist who targets vulnerable women with pathetic scams,' said Shades matter-of-factly, 'then yes, she did. A field agent is duty-bound to inform her superiors of all information that may be relevant to her mission.'

'Sorry, Cas,' said Lori, he thought sympathetically.

'No, no. What have you got to be sorry about? It's true. I wish it wasn't.' He looked to Shades. 'I guess you must think I'm a bit of a lowlife, huh, Ms Carmody? If you want to hand me over to the cops, I won't blame you. If you want to set one of your mind-wipe teams on me again, I won't resist this time, I know there are bigger things than me going on. But I just want to tell you – both of you – that you don't *need* to mind-wipe me. I won't breathe a word about you or your organisation's existence to *anyone*, I promise. And I mean it.' He dared a grin. 'Not even those guys with the big cheques from the National Inquirer.'

'Cas . . .' said Lori, he hoped affectionately.

'All right, Casino,' intruded Shades. 'Your Damascene conversion from minor criminal to upstanding, self-sacrificing citizen is an inspiration to us all –' Cas shot a look at Lori, mouthed *Damascene?* – 'and the manner in which you undeniably assisted Lori last night suggests it might even be genuine. Besides, the situation has moved on. Wolf Judson knows who you are now. Mind-wiping you or placing you in conventional custody are both courses of action that might well endanger your life, certainly more than allowing you to stay here under our protection until the present matter is resolved. It seems, Casino, that for the moment at least, you are one of us.'

'That's great,' Casino smiled. 'I mean, thank you, Ms Carmody, I appreciate it. I know you could have . . . the old wash your hands routine. Lori, I don't know what to . . . one of *who*, exactly?'

'Angel Blue has permission to divulge whatever information she believes to be necessary to ensure your continued safety,' said Shades.

'Angel *who*?'

Lori gave a little wave. 'Over here. It's kind of a work name.'

Casino shook his head. 'Before you start divulging, I think I'm going to need coffee.'

A tech entered the room before the discussion got as far as decaf or latte. A tech with a print-out in his hand and an 'I know something you're going to want to know too' expression on his otherwise unmemorable face.

'Results, Agent Angel,' he said.

'Thanks, Carter.' Lori took the print-out and she and Shades scrutinised it together.

'Results of what?' Casino didn't want to be left out. 'I mean, if this is necessary to ensure my continued safety stuff. If not, I can always . . .' He gestured vaguely outside.

'Results of feeding certain names into our data banks and searching for connections,' Lori said. 'The names I was downloading from Pettinger's computer last night before I was rudely interrupted.'

'But didn't Judson take your disk – along with everything else?'

Lori smiled at Casino's bemusement. But then, he wasn't to know that her training at Spy High had included memory enhancement techniques. 'That wasn't a problem.'

'So, what? Are these guys all related or something?'

'Kind of.' Lori scanned the names again. Allenby. Kreuser. Lashman. Pound. Dane Stockdale. Names like pieces in a jigsaw puzzle. They were beginning to fit, though the overall picture remained unclear. 'Twenty men. All of them served in the security services in one capacity or another. All of them are now officially deceased. Wheelless accident. Mountaineering accident. Drowned while sailing his boat. Killed in a light aircraft crash.'

'You'd have thought security service guys would be able to take better care of themselves,' opined Casino, 'or are you saying you don't reckon these deaths were accidental?'

Lori remembered a night not long ago at the Sleepwell Cemetery. 'We have persuasive evidence to suggest that these "deaths" aren't even that. And there's another link between them, too, so it seems. Over a period of five years, they all worked in an anti-terrorist agency under the guidance and leadership of one Chase Judson. Sound familiar?'

'Don't tell me. Wolf's . . . brother?'

'Exactly. His older brother.'

'I'd heard he had one but –' Casino frowned – 'isn't he supposed to be dead?'

'Exactly again. Tragically killed during a routine training exercise.'

'Yeah, yeah,' Casino paused her, 'I'm getting the hang of this. But you don't think he's dead either, right?'

'I think he's very much alive,' Lori stated grimly. 'Luanne?'

Shades nodded in agreement. 'We need to inform Mr Deveraux.'

'So all the people who are supposed to be dead, they're actually still alive?' Casino shook his head. 'It's a crazy kind of world you people live in.'

'You get used to it, Cas,' Lori encouraged, 'eventually.'

'And your conclusion, Lori?' Shades redirected her protégé to the business at hand.

Lori's expression grew colder again. 'I think Chase Judson's alive. I think Dane Stockdale and the others are alive. I think their deaths were faked. I think Wolf

Judson ordered special animates to be constructed by Pettinger and substituted them in their place. I think wherever they are, they're together, and whatever they're doing, it's not good. Bottom line, Luanne? I think they're planning to assassinate the President of the United States.'

EIGHT

They sent a tech team into Action Animates under the guise of a full-scale inquiry by the Animate Regulation Enforcement Board following 'reports of serious breaches in the proprieties of animate construction'. Wilford Pettinger was not at work: the little man who rather fearfully welcomed the investigators and put himself and the company at their disposal introduced himself as the assistant managing director and no, he had no idea as to the whereabouts of his superior. Pettinger was not at his house, either; Deveraux had it under surveillance. The security staff who were mustered for inspection at Action Animates were entirely different from those who'd shot at Lori and Casino the previous night. Tie cameras worn by the techs allowed Angel Blue to establish that. And early evidence pointed to total compliance with accepted safety standards in animate manufacture. It was clear that tracks had been covered here, and covered well.

Like Pettinger, Wolf Judson seemed reluctant to appear in public that day. He certainly wasn't at the

Eden. Surveillance was being carried out on his house too, but there was no question of a move against him at this stage. 'There's no proof of any wrongdoing,' Shades pointed out. Casino thought his sore ribs suggested otherwise, but the field handler was adamant. They'd get to Wolf soon enough. In the meantime, she'd sent for an expert on the Judsons to more fully brief Lori as to the family's history.

Lori was pleased. Anything was preferable to standing around doing nothing, even a lecture from somebody who wouldn't know one end of a shock blaster from the other. She was pleased until she learned who the Deveraux 'expert' actually was.

Jake.

As dark, as broodingly magnetic as ever. He didn't look like he'd used a comb since Simon's memorial ceremony.

'Lori,' he said, 'how are you?'

'I'm surviving,' she said. Without you, she thought. 'You?'

'The same.'

'And you're Mr Human Encyclopaedia when it comes to the Judson family.'

'I did my first year holo-project on the history of firearms, majoring in American manufacturers including the Judsons. I'm surprised you weren't aware of that, Lori. Though in the first year, I guess you were more interested in *Ben*'s holo-project.'

'I think that's fifteen-all,' said Casino from the far side of the motel room. 'If we're scoring.'

Jake seemed to notice him for the first time. It was just the three of them in the room. 'Who are you?'

'Robbie Royal.' He got up and approached Jake, hand outstretched. 'My friends call me Cas. As in Casino.'

'I'll bear it in mind,' grudged Jake. His eyes flickered between this idiot with the dumb name and the lopsided grin and Lori. He wondered.

Cas withdrew his hand unshaken. 'So. And you are . . .?'

'Jake Daly,' supplied Lori. 'One of my fellow team members from my training days.'

She didn't say 'and ex-boyfriend with whom there are still unresolved tensions', but Casino could deduce that for himself. His confidence tricks had tutored him ably in the analysis of voice tone and body language. If Black-Haired and Brooding had been with Lori in the Garden of Eden, they wouldn't have needed to uproot a camera to start a fire. Jake Daly, he registered. As in watch your back, Cas, this guy isn't going to *like* you.

'Is he security cleared?' Jake demanded of Lori. 'What's he doing here?'

'Yes, thank you for being so concerned,' returned Lori, 'and Cas is *involved* in this mission now. He's risked his life. He probably saved mine.'

'Who hasn't?' grunted Jake.

Casino thought he ought to step in there with some witty or cutting response, but if this Jake was half as useful with his fists as Lori, maybe he'd better wait for a more advantageous opening. Never bet all your money on the *first* throw of the dice. Besides, Shades was now entering. Personal matters could be put to one side.

'Did you bring your disk?' she asked of Jake. He had. A holo-disk, capable of projecting a three-dimensional presentation in sound and vision through an appropriately equipped computer.

He slotted it into the computer now, initiated the program. 'I made a few revisions on the plane,' he said, 'deletions, mainly, so we focus only on the Judsons. And I've removed the original voice track. I'll talk you through the key points live so we don't waste time.'

'Can we still hope for sound effects?' said Casino.

'Oh, yes,' said Jake.

And the room exploded with gunfire. And it surged with sudden soldiers, gangsters, cops. They were all around them, all armed, shooting, charging, shouting and dying. Two hundred years of battle and war crammed into seconds, a hundred men and more into a single small room. A World War II GI was storming a German machine gun emplacement by Casino's side, his own weapon clattering hectically in Cas's ear. The Seventh Cavalry were in full pursuit of the Sioux and it didn't look like the motel-room door was going to stop them.

'Jake, adjust the scope, I think,' advised Shades. 'We don't want to startle any other guests.'

There weren't any, but the field handler's point was a good one. Jake keyed in an adjustment to the range of the holo-projection. The figures and the fighting confined themselves to a nimbus of violence in the centre of the room, barely touching their audience.

'So,' commenced Jake, 'the Judson company is one of the most significant and renowned manufacturers of arms today. The Judson name has been forever associated with conflicts from the days of the Old West to the present cutting-edge weaponry of our elite special forces. But how did it all start?'

From the general melee a lone visual image emerged – a man in the uniform of a Union Army officer, Civil War period, a man with a drooping moustache, hands clasped behind him, brow furrowed in deep thought as he picked his way across a battlefield of corpses. 'Irving Judson, the founder of the family fortune. Irving fought in the early years of the Civil War and was allegedly horrified by what he saw. Not by the scale of the slaughter, I'm afraid, but by its inefficiency. "We live in an industrial age," he's reported to have said. "Death must be industrialised, too." So after he was wounded at Gettysburg and invalided out of active duty, Irving set about making his own contribution to the business of war. He began designing and building firearms.'

The scene cut to Irving Judson, still heavily moustachioed but now in civilian attire, gazing down the barrel of a rifle and stroking its gleaming metal length almost lovingly. 'Rifles, revolvers, fixed guns, handguns, the type didn't matter to Irving, only that their sights were accurate, their loading and firing mechanisms reliable, and that they could kill more people more quickly than any other weapons on the market. He was a driven man, devoted to his work. Even so, he still found time to father nine children. The marriage was rumoured to have been a shotgun wedding. The joke went, only because Irving thought he was marrying the shotgun.'

'Did you make that up, Jake?' said Lori.

Irving Judson faded into a succession of bearded, stetsoned and long-coated frontier types, all of them demonstrating their prowess with either rifle or handgun. 'Old Irving made his mark, all right. Sadly for him, the Civil War ended before he was really into production, but there were other wars to be fought, and as the West opened up – the age of the gunfighter – demand for the Judson repeating rifle and the Judson .45 calibre revolver escalated. In their day these guns were as famous as the Winchester rifle or the Colt .45, and they shot dead just as many people. When Irving died in 1906 at the age of eighty, he'd let it be known that his only regret in what he considered to be a generally fulfilled and productive life was that he'd never managed to surpass the gatling-gun in terms of sheer killing efficiency. They buried him with enough firepower to storm the Pearly Gates by himself.'

'So the little Judsons had plenty to live up to,' commented Casino. 'With ancestors like that, no wonder Wolf's a fruitcake.'

Jake regarded him humourlessly as the twentieth century unfolded before them. 'They did their best,' he continued. 'They followed in their father's footsteps. Wherever there was violence throughout the 1900s, there was a Judson. Not physically, of course, but in spirit. In the cold steel of guns and the relentless rattle of ammunition, in the blood and the screams and the fear of dying men. In the trenches of the Great War. In the murders and mayhem of the Roaring Twenties. At Pearl Harbour. At Midway. At Iwo Jima. On the beaches of Normandy. At the fall of Hitler. In the disaster of Vietnam. In the War on Terror.' A choreography of combat unfolded before them. 'There's always been war. I guess there always will be. Which means in a sense the Judsons will always be with us.'

'The way things are going,' muttered Casino, not too loudly but loudly enough, 'so will this presentation.'

Jake glared. 'Coming up to date,' he said pointedly, 'the Judson company has diversified in recent decades, particularly under the stewardship of Wolf's late father, Washington Judson.' Law enforcement officers in body armour and wielding what appeared to be laser pistols scrambled among the ruins of a city. 'The emphasis of both design and production has shifted to weapons of urban warfare, the Judson pacifier that you can see in use here – the Judson Jolt as it's been nicknamed – being the most famous example, a staple of police forces nationwide since the riots of the 2020s.

'And so to the latest and perhaps final generation of the Judson family. Washington had three children. The oldest, Chase –' a more closely-shaven version of Wolf appeared before them, bereft of pony-tail but complete with pacifier – 'Wolf who you've met –' looking exactly as he had in the Eden two nights ago – 'and the youngest, a daughter, Diana.' According to the hologram, Diana was very much the youngest, barely out of her teens. Blonde, muscular, almost masculine, and visibly ingrained with her brothers' arrogance.

'A bit of an after-thought, was she?' Casino wondered.

'Partly,' Jake said, 'but she's actually ten years older than this now, if she's alive.'

'If she's alive?' Lori probed alertly.

'It's why I said this could be the *final* generation of Judsons. Wolf has no children that we know of, Chase is dead—'

'Hah!' crowed Cas.

Jake regarded him with near open hostility. 'What do you mean, *hah*?'

'I'll explain later, Jake,' soothed Lori. 'Go on.'

'Chase is dead,' he resumed reluctantly, 'leaving no offspring. And apparently there was a huge family row back in the mid-fifties which led to Diana Judson doing a vanishing act. She disappeared completely. Not been seen since, so far as anybody knows. She could be dead, too.'

'I think we should carry out a data-search on Diana Judson, Luanne,' Lori said to Shades, 'don't you? Just to be on the safe side.'

Shades nodded her agreement. 'I'll tell the techs.'

'Why? What's going on?' Jake didn't like it that Robbie Casino or whatever he was called seemed to be more up to speed on Lori's assignment than he was. 'Is there a problem with Wolf Judson?'

'If there was,' Lori posed, 'what kind of enemy do you think he'd be, Jake?'

'One you'd sooner not *have* as an enemy, Lori, that's for sure. The weaponry may have changed over the years, but the Judson mind-set hasn't. One reason old Irving became the favourite he did with the western settlers and frontiersmen was because he believed in the pioneering spirit himself – passionately. As fiercely as he believed that a good gun was one that killed the maximum amount of people in the minimum amount of time. Self-determination, the right to bear arms and to use those arms as you see fit, that's the Judson way. As far as old Irving was concerned, guns made the law, and he made the guns. There was no higher authority. The Judsons have always regarded government with contempt, kind of an infringement on their liberty, even when supplying our armies with munitions. You just get the feeling they wouldn't really care which side's men were killed by them. So,' Jake considered, 'what kind of enemy would Wolf be, Lori? Seriously? Ruthless, selfish, focussed. One who wouldn't rest until he'd destroyed you. One who wouldn't stop until you were dead.'

'So you're studying the wolf's lair,' said Casino. 'It sure beats a hole in the ground, doesn't it?'

After Jake's briefing on the Judsons, Luanne Carmody had asked – politely – that Cas leave the room while she and the two teenagers discussed 'operational matters'. Cas had said he had an operational matter to sort out himself with the vending machine at the end of the corridor. He'd sunk several plastic cups-worth of equally plastic coffee until Luanne and Jake had departed the room too. Then he'd sidled back in.

He wanted a word with Lori alone.

A new holo-disk was playing. This one generating the image of a visually stunning building that almost seemed to be growing out of the wall of the Grand Canyon. The scale was such that Casino could see the canyon rim above and the winding Colorado River far below. The building's brickwork was styled and stained after the colour and grains of the surrounding natural rock. Its centrepiece, however, its most daring and magnificent architectural innovation, was the twin terraces that swept out from the wall to overhang thin air in bold semi-circles – defining both the higher and lower limits of the property. Between them, the canyon wall was studded with one-way windows. No entrances or exits, access to these rooms was via elevator or spiral staircase from the remainder of the house built more conventionally above ground some distance from the lip of the canyon.

Casino recognised the construction at once. He'd seen pictures and read about it in magazines. Wolf Judson lived there.

'There are some interesting features that I'm sure the general public doesn't know about,' said Lori. 'For one thing, the whole place's shielded against surveillance. We can't see inside, not even with our satellites, not even with infra-red, x-ray or heat signature probes. Wolf could be in there or he might not. He's pulled the curtains on us.'

'But you're going to find out, right?' Casino was learning how Lori's organisation worked.

'I'm going to pay our friend Mr Judson a little visit, yes.' Lori's eyes gleamed. 'To thank him for his hospitality last night.'

'You mean, you're just gonna walk in there and give him another chance to kill you?'

Lori regarded Casino defensively. 'I'm not exactly "just gonna walk in there", Cas. I'm not that easy to kill, as plenty of others before Wolf have found out. You don't *know*.'

'But I'll lay odds that Jake knows, doesn't he? I'll lay odds Jake knows a lot more about you than I do.'

'Of course he does, Cas,' Lori said. 'I told you, we trained together.'

'A little extra-curricular activity as well, I'm betting.' Cas was also trying not to sound jealous. He wasn't quite making it.

Lori sighed. She should have seen this coming. When two boys and one girl were gathered together . . . 'Jake and I used to be together, yes,' she admitted, 'but not any more. I'm not actually seeing anybody right now . . .' She didn't know why she'd added that last unnecessary snippet of information. A hint, maybe?

'Lori, I don't know.' Casino ran his hands through his hair which made it spikier than ever, like it was anxious about something.

'What, Cas?' Lori prompted. 'What don't you know?'

'Everything. What's going on. What's happening to my life. Lori, this is all heavy stuff. I mean, the kind of stuff you're into, it's heavy. Even if we ignore glowering ex-boyfriends who look like they'd be happy to finish what Wolf started as far as Robbie Royal's concerned, there's your whole line of work. There's the putting your life on the line, which I take it is like an every day occur-rence for you, like eating a cheeseburger. There's the things like "and he won't stop until you're dead" dropped into the conversation with as little fuss as if it was a weather report. And there's everything that happened to us last night. Maybe that's water off a duck's back to you, Lori, but to me that's like, woah, time out. What am I getting *into*?'

'What are you saying, Cas?' She knew. The disap-pointment was in her already.

Casino shook his head apologetically. 'I'm just a small-time crook. I fleece tourists. I scam them. I do dodgy deals. I'm a street hustler. I'm not proud of any of that but you can't change your bet after the race has been run. But I want . . . I think I want something more, and I *thought*, maybe there was something for me in your world, Lori, something good. And at first it just seemed kind of exciting, but now I don't know if I can cope with all this, with how you live, with the danger . . . I *want* to be able to because I think, well, I *know*, I like you, Lori, but . . .' He shrugged wretchedly. 'Maybe the mind-wipe was a better idea after all.'

So, Lori pondered gloomily, score one for Jake and Ben. They might have been tiresomely intense and unremitting at times, but at least they had commitment, belief in a cause. Not to have that, not to have the strength and the courage to stand up and fight for what you believed was right, that made you somehow less than complete, less than you were meant to be, less than you *should* be.

But hey, that was just her opinion. And to be fair, Casino had asked for none of this. He'd stumbled into her life. Maybe it *was* better that he should just stumble out again. But she hoped not. 'I can't tell you what to do, Cas,' she said. 'They're getting my SkyBike ready and I've got to go. We'll talk when I get back. One thing I will say now, though. Your own words – sometimes you've just got to roll the dice and take a chance. Are you up to it, Casino Royal? Go on, roll 'em. See what happens.'

It was only after Lori had left, SkyBiking her way towards the Judson residence in the Grand Canyon, that Daly confronted him. Cas supposed the dark and scowling secret agent hadn't wanted an unseemly brawl to develop anywhere within her presence. Luanne Carmody and the techs were monitoring Lori's progress in one of the rooms. Jake had Cas all to himself by the vending machine.

'You want one of these?' Cas offered him the cup of

coffee he'd just received. 'I don't recommend it, but they are kind of addictive.'

'You buy that with your own money, Casino?' snorted Jake. 'Or with cash pilfered from a widow from Idaho?'

'Neither, actually.' Cas watched the other boy warily. 'Bearing in mind my own clothes and wallet were lost in the course of duty, this is a loan from the wonderful organisation you work for.' The coffee was tongue-skinningly hot. If Daly made any kind of violent move, a cupful in the face was likely to slow him down.

'Yeah, that'd be right. Leeching off somebody else. Lori's told me all about you now, Robbie. I'm not impressed.'

'Has she? And aren't you? And is the Robbie reference to prove you're not a friend or that you're as deaf as a post and didn't hear me properly before?'

'You tried to rob Lori, didn't you?' Jake pressed menacingly. 'That doesn't sit well with me.'

'What are you, her guard-dog? Lori can look after herself. She doesn't need any growling ex-boyfriend to fight her corner for her. Yeah, Jake,' retaliated Casino, 'Lori's told me a little bit about you, too. What's the deal? Realising you made a mistake and hoping you'll get back together? That's one bet *I* won't be placing, Jakey boy.'

Before he realised it, Cas found himself slammed back against the vending machine with the potential weapon of his coffee spilled to the floor and Jake's forearm pressed across his windpipe. 'You fancy your chances with Lori, do you, Casino?' The strangled croak that came as an answer could have been yes, no, maybe, or even the beginning of let go, you're throttling me. Jake, apparently, didn't care. 'You think you're man enough for Lori, do you? You think she'd even look twice at a no-good jail-bait loser like you? What's that, Casino? Maybe I'm deaf as a post. I can't *hear* you.'

Much to Cas's relief, Jake eased the pressure on his throat. Just. 'I said *you* must think so, Daly,' he gasped, 'otherwise why come on like the hard man? Is this you, like, warning me off? A letter would have done, or can't you write?'

'You think you're pretty smart, don't you?' Jake brought his sneer very close to Casino's face. Though he was younger, he was taller, broader. 'You're a little fish in a little pond, and I'm wondering if I should be the one to let the water out.'

'That bad breath of yours, Jake, is that supposed to be a secret weapon or what?'

Jake grinned coldly. He took a step back, let go of Casino. 'You're not worth my time or trouble,' he dismissed, 'and you won't be worth Lori's, either. As soon as this business with Judson is over, we'll go back to where we belong and you'll go back to where you belong – the gutter. She'll have forgotten you in a week. "Casino" Royal? Who'd put their money on you?'

Jake's contempt stung. The worst thing was, some of it was well-founded. 'Yeah, well, why don't I make your day and leave early?'

'What?'

'Leave? It's only a single syllable. Thought it *might* have made your vocabulary, big man. It means walk out the door. And early? Like *now*. Tell Lori I'm sorry I missed her.' Casino stalked off down the corridor.

'Wait. You can't go.' Jake intercepted him. 'It's too

dangerous for you out there at the moment. You *have* to stay with us.'

'Jake,' Cas retorted, pushing him aside, 'I didn't know you cared. And I've got news for you. I *don't*.'

He half-expected Daly to attempt some kind of physical restraint, or maybe just to beat him senseless for his own good, but he did nothing. And Cas was out of the door and into the late afternoon Las Vegas sun, and he was running down the street feeling sickness and shame inside. He was running hard and he never looked back and he hadn't a clue where he was going.

For the greasy proprietor of the Heartbrake Motel, life was good. He hadn't been so busy for years, not since before his wife had left and taken the concept of 'rooms as clean as your own home' with her. These new people, they paid up front and didn't seem to notice he was charging double the normal rates. Feds. Even the black woman with the shades and the kids – okay, maybe not the one he'd just seen racing by like somebody was after him with a gun, but the others – they were Feds for sure. He could smell 'em a mile off, even with all the other odours around here. Fried chicken going cold, for example, food too good to waste.

The proprietor returned to his inner office to finish his meal. He'd have done better to stay there. But he was a businessman, after a fashion. When the bell rang minutes later, he went to answer it.

More money, he thought, when he saw the three men in black suits and blacker sunglasses waiting at the desk.

'Afternoon, gennlemen,' he greeted them between slurps of his fingers. 'What c'n I do for youse?'

'You can die,' said the first gennleman, which probably wasn't an answer the proprietor was expecting. It was all he got, however.

That, and a bullet.

He should have gone after Royal immediately, Jake knew that. He should have twisted his arm up behind his back – a therapeutic, stress-reducing bonus – and marched him to one of their rooms and locked him in. He should have done *something*. What he'd said was true: outside of their protection, Casino was not only in possible personal jeopardy, which Jake tried to kid himself he could live with, but could also compromise the integrity of Lori's entire mission.

Because, in the end, this was *Lori*'s mission, not his. He was risking ruining it for her, maybe endangering her safety. What if the bad guys somehow caught up with Royal and he told them where Lori was . . .

Jake swore at himself. He'd allowed his dislike of Robbie Royal to cloud his judgement. He'd let anger take him over. It was happening more and more these days and he needed to do something about it. Maybe go see the Deveraux emotion management consultant at Spy High. Maybe.

After he'd stopped cooling his heels by the vending machine and tracked down Casino.

He didn't get as far as the front desk. Not after he saw the dead proprietor lolling in his chair and three armed men in black heading his way.

Jake didn't delay now. With a burst of sleepshot he

eliminated the first, retreated back into the motel as the man's companions opened fire.

It looked like Casino would have to wait.

Eventually, of course, he had to *stop* running. You couldn't keep going for ever, even if you wanted to.

Casino sagged against a wall and sucked in great gulps of air as if he'd just surfaced from an ocean in which he'd all but drowned. That was how he felt even with the oxygen in his lungs. Drowning. Out of his depth. All at sea.

In too deep.

Too deep? What was he thinking? That he couldn't simply return to his old life, get back to the lobbies and the lonely women and the package with the broken vase? That there was no way back? That he was committed?

Commitment and Casino. They might begin with the same letter, but that was about all they had in common.

A wheelless drew up alongside. A recent model with one-way windows. Casino hoped they weren't going to ask him directions. He only had a vague idea himself where in town he was.

The rear window lowered. A man in a black suit and sunglasses smiled at him. 'Excuse me, excuse me . . .'

'Sorry, man,' Casino shrugged, moving towards the wheelless, 'if you want to know where you're heading down here I have absolutely no idea.'

'Oh, we know precisely where we're heading,' smiled the man with the sunglasses. And the gun. 'And you're coming with us.'

❊

It was dusk by the time Lori reached the Grand Canyon on her SkyBike. She was skimming above bare, flat Arizona desert land, miles of monotony in every direction, and then suddenly, without warning, the ground opened up like a jagged, gaping wound and she was plunging into the canyon. The stabiliser controls on her bike were neither fazed nor impressed by geological phenomena, however striking they were to human eyes. Lori might have been startled by the magnificence of the canyon, its proud walls reddened by the setting sun, the abrupt and incredible drop below her to the ribbon of the Colorado River, the way the rock seemed to fling itself above her head as if it was growing at a rate of hundreds of feet a second, Nature's skyscraper, but all the time the SkyBike's systems simply calculated distance from the surface and recalibrated height and trajectory accordingly. Machines, Lori thought ruefully, had no *soul*.

It was almost a mile to the canyon floor.

And as the red rock parapets closed out the sun, darkness seemed to ooze from the stony ground and the canyon became a well, a pit. That was good. Lori did not even consider activating the SkyBike's light beam. The navigator function would take her unerringly to Wolf Judson's house irrespective of light or darkness. It would be an advantage if she was not seen. She was not likely to be a welcome visitor.

Night had risen fully from the canyon floor by the time Lori sighted her destination – the glow of rows of lights a thousand metres above her. She landed the bike a little way from Wolf's home and deactivated it. For the time being at least, its work was done. She stripped off the clothes it would have been acceptable for the general public to see her wearing and wriggled into a chameleon suit. Infra-red viewing panels working: no need for a flash-light to find her way around. Gloves and boots treated with clingskin: it was going to be a heck of a climb.

Now, what might Wolf be hiding in his modest desert retreat?

Lori scaled the canyon wall quickly, expertly. It was no obstacle. Back at Spy High, they'd trained with clingskin by climbing sheer surfaces that tipped and moved, that actively tried to shake them off. The Grand Canyon had been around millennia too long to concern itself with the actions of a single slim girl clad in black. Before long, she'd gained the lower of the Judson building's two terraces.

She hauled herself over the safety wall. The terrace described an arch but ahead of her, flat against the side of the canyon, were the windows and doors, probably glasteel, that would provide her with access to the house's interior, and hopefully to material evidence of Wolf's wrongdoing, whatever form that might take. Maybe Casino and Vegas generally were getting to her. She'd put *money* on it being a plot against the president.

She wouldn't show up on either of the spy cameras, placed like tired eyes at both ends of the terrace. Neither would the deactivator that she used to disable the doors' locks. The cameras were directed outwards. They couldn't notice the doors opening in.

Lori entered a long, rectangular room. It was in darkness and empty. Of furniture. Of people. Maybe Wolf was moving out. Warily, Lori padded forward.

The doors buzzed as they closed behind her.

The lights came on.

So did a plasma screen set into the wall to her left. Wolf Judson was displaying his teeth for her benefit. He could *see* her.

And the men, the four men bulging into the room through its only other door, all dressed incongruously in black suits, *they* could see her too.

'Welcome, Ms Angel,' said Wolf Judson. 'We've been expecting you.'

And the men were on her. Lori deflected the first blow, the second, ducked low for the third to swing harmlessly above her and kicked back to reduce that particular assailant to one functioning knee-cap. In almost the same motion she turned, kicked again.

Three to go.

'Is this how you greet all your guests, Judson?' Such close quarters. Sleepshot no advantage. And why had her chameleon suit failed?

'Only those who seek to oppose me, my dear. Only my enemies.'

'That's me on both counts,' Lori admitted.

Attacks came from right and left. Lori balanced on one leg. As they lunged, she kicked right, punched left. Then grabbed her final foe by his lapels. Fell backwards. Thrust her feet up, into his stomach. He hit the floor and stayed there.

'Well if that's the best you can offer, Judson, I'd give up now.' Lori was scarcely breathing faster. She drew her shock blaster from its holster. 'It's not one of yours, I'm afraid, but it'll do.'

Wolf seemed unaffected by his minions' defeat. 'Please,' he said, 'Lori, take off that rather unflattering hood. Let me see who I'm talking to. You must have gathered that your suit's usefulness is at an end, in any case.'

True enough. Lori had nothing to lose by removing her chameleon suit's hood. She took hold of it under her chin, peeled it off over her head to hang down her back. 'So how did you manage to detect me?'

'Oh, please,' sniffed Wolf, 'I have scientists working for me, too. For reimbursement rather more generous than I imagine your organisation offers. They analysed the suit we relieved you of before, divined its function, developed counter-measures. Some kind of blocking device, I understand. As soon as you entered my property, it recognised the nano-chip signature of your suit and neutralised it. The invisible rendered visible.'

'So what now?' Lori said. She glanced towards the terrace doors. Maybe she ought to get out while she could. The wisdom of Shades: there is no dishonour in retreat when the alternative is a death that will accomplish nothing.

'I advise you *not* to think about leaving quite yet, Lori.' Wolf's smile was that of a hyena who had chanced upon a corpse with plenty of meat still on the bones.

His tone, though, warned her to pause. 'No? Why not?'

'No,' Wolf said. 'I advise you to remove your wristbands and your belt, and place them on the floor in front of you. Your shock blaster can keep them company as well, I think.'

'Now why would I want to give up my only weapons?' Lori challenged.

Wolf Judson chuckled, like ice cubes dropped into a

glass. 'Because I advise you to follow my instructions exactly, my dear. I think you'll want to. Because if you *don't*, then something very nasty will happen in front of your eyes to someone I think you'd sooner see unharmed.'

'What are you talking about, Judson?'

The camera on Wolf pulled back. Lori saw for the first time that he was seated on some kind of marble throne in a room otherwise as featureless and bare as the one she was in. She saw that he was accompanied by only one other person, and that this other person was kneeling with his hands tied behind his back and the rope looped and fastened around the arm of the throne. She recognised him, and the recognition made her groan with inner despair.

Casino Royal was Wolf's captive.

NINE

He yelled to her not to listen. He shouted at her to go, to save herself, that he didn't matter. But of course Casino *did* matter. Of course, she *had* to listen to Wolf Judson.

And she did what he told her to do.

A little pile of weapons lay among the bodies of the beaten men. 'I draw the line at putting on another of those fig-leaf bikinis, though.' Make a joke. Ignore troubling questions such as how Judson had located Cas and what that might mean for Shades and Jake. Sound confident. Wait for Wolf to make the mistake that the bad guys always did.

Hope that it would come soon.

'I have plasma screens throughout my home, Lori. I'm going to use them to guide you to where I want you to be. Deviate from my directions just once and your unimpressive friend's breath will deviate from his body, permanently. Do you understand?'

Lori did. At least Wolf leading her through the cold spartan corridors of his house granted her a better idea of its layout. 'Nice place you've got here, Judson,' she said. 'It's really *you*.' Austere, metallic, remote. 'About as warm and homely as a tomb.'

'Creature comforts have never been my priority,' said Wolf. 'Luxury is the prerequisite of decadence. Only men who are less than men desire it. Left here. Good. Continue to the elevator at the end of the corridor.'

'Elevator? No stairs? A bit decadent, isn't it? I thought only men who are less than men chose an elevator instead of stairs.' Goad him if possible. Annoy him into losing his concentration.

'Ah,' countered Wolf Judson, 'but this elevator has a specific purpose. It will take you to a very special part of my home. I will control it from here, by the way. Simply step inside.' Lori obeyed and the door slid shut behind her. There was a screen even here. 'When I first had this dwelling built, before my plans took rather a different turn, one floor was set aside to be a museum open to the public.' The elevator hummed upwards. 'A museum that would celebrate and immortalise the achievements of my family since the days of Irving Judson himself.'

'What? You were going to have the names inscribed on the walls of all the people your guns had killed in 200 years, were you? You'd need a lot of walls.'

'You disappoint me, Lori,' tutted Wolf, 'a young lady so proficient in the use of firearms. Yet why should I be surprised? You are the product of a society too cowardly to acknowledge that it is only the power of weapons that keeps it strong. I still hear talk from time to time of coalition and cooperation among nations as being the "right" way forward. Nonsense, of course. *Might* makes right. And guns make might.'

'And *you* make the guns. Well done,' added Lori sarcastically.

'And soon our guns will remake the world.' Wolf seemed unable to recognise irony. Lori was not surprised. The kind of lunatics she'd faced since joining Spy High were not big on humour or self-deprecation. 'But I rush ahead of myself.' As the elevator slid to a stop and the door did not open. 'I was speaking of the museum. Only four galleries were completed before I abandoned the project. Very few people have seen them. Even fewer have lived to talk about them.'

'Well let's hope I make it even fewer plus one,' said Lori.

Wolf smiled almost approvingly, a rictus of the lips that nauseated her more than any other expression so far. 'You have spirit, girl,' he acknowledged. 'You remind me of my sister. Almost a pity to see it wasted.'

The elevator doors opened. Lori found herself gazing down the single sun-baked street of a town from the Old West. It was lined with saloons punctuated by a mercantile store, a barber's shop, an undertaker's. At the far end was a door, presently closed, set into a wall otherwise displaying a holographic representation of the Arizona desert. The stripped-in sky suggested High Noon. Animate townsfolk stood petrified on the raised wooden sidewalk or in the street itself. Lying on the ground outside the elevator were a Judson .45 calibre revolver and a Judson repeating rifle, gleaming in the unreal sun. Lying some fifty metres further on, as still and as lifeless as the animates, was Wilford Pettinger, rifle and revolver spilled from his twisted dead fingers.

'Still playing games,' Lori muttered.

'Very deadly games, I assure you,' qualified Wolf. 'My gambling friends are not with me today, so I have the pleasure of viewing your struggle for survival all to myself.'

'Did you get some kicks out of watching Pettinger as well?' scorned Lori.

'Not really,' sighed Wolf. 'As you can see, he didn't get far. The rewards for success are high at Judson, but so is the price of failure, and Pettinger ought really to have apprehended you more cleanly the other night. But I have no doubt that you will last for longer than he, Lori, my dear, a *little* longer. Let me explain the rules. Four galleries, as I mentioned, each dedicated to an historical period in which the Judson brand flourished. All you have to do is proceed through them and reach the door that opens on to the *next* gallery. Child's play. You even have appropriate weaponry to help you.'

'If it's child's play,' said Lori, 'why do I need appropriate weaponry to help me?'

'You don't want me to answer that, do you?' smirked Judson.

'And when I make it through the fourth gallery, what then?'

'*When* you make it? Ah, the optimism of youth, so often defeated by experience.' Wolf Judson waxed lyrical. '*If* you make it, in the final gallery your idiot boyfriend and myself will be waiting. Attempt any other means of reaching us, however, and Casino will *not* be alive to greet you. The animates will be activated the instant you set foot in the gallery.' A final predatory leer. 'I shan't insult you by wishing you good luck.'

'Don't worry about it, Wolfie.' Lori glanced right and

left, to the swing-doors of saloons, to windows, to roof-tops. She thought of the Gun Run, a staple of Spy High training. She'd been good at the Gun Run. 'Luck I won't need. See you soon.'

And she was into her stride at once, darting forward, scooping up her prescribed weapons. Two hands, two guns. She was going to need them.

To her right, a brace of cowboys broke from a saloon, six-guns blazing. Too slow, like their animate gears were rusting. Her Judson .45 sent them spilling headlong into the street even as the smashing of glass from the upper hotel windows on her left made her swing her rifle that way. One-handed rifle firing: you aimed a little higher than usual to allow for the recoil. The rifle spat twice. Two bodies tumbling to the sidewalk.

There was crossfire now as Lori raced into the centre of the street. She dived forward, hot lead flashing past her ears, placed her latest assailants as she rolled, then right-side up gunned them down with deadly, superlative accuracy.

She was on one knee now, the rifle braced against her shoulder. She spied a glint of metal on the rooftop. Fired. A gunman pitched forward and dropped into a water butt.

An undertaker and his assistant charged from their premises firing wildly, looking to rustle up some business. Lori's trusty .45 ensured that they did, even though they wouldn't be able to handle it themselves.

And then the dancing girls opened fire forcing Lori to roll over in the dust before she could retaliate. When she did, she didn't miss.

Neither could she wait around. Her strike-rate was

high but speed was likely to be the decisive survival
factor. The less time she spent in each gallery, the less
time the animates had to get lucky. Lori scrambled to her
feet, backed swiftly towards the door to the second
gallery, firing steadily. She didn't plan on doing a Wild
Bill Hickok and catching a slug between the shoulder-
blades.

Then, all at once, the animates were silent and still
again, those whose neutralised bodies did not already
litter the street. Lori realised she must have passed a
general environment deactivation point. She was safe. So
long as Wolf Judson played the game by his own rules.

She didn't drop her guard or turn her back until she
physically reached the door. A quarter of the way to
Casino.

Breathing in deeply, Lori passed through.

Into sweat and smoke and the fumes of strong drink
and the sounds of ragtime from a piano in the corner,
barely audible above the raised voices and laughter of a
cram of people having a Good Time. A uniquely 1920s
kind of Good Time. In the 1920s, alcohol was outlawed
in the United States – Prohibition, they called it. Lori
remembered from her twentieth-century history
modules. It didn't stop people from drinking, however, it
just assisted in the creation of a new breed of illegal
establishment where they could go and drink. The
Speakeasy.

Lori was in one now.

She scanned the club for signs of danger. Speakeasies
tended to be owned by mobsters who made their fortune
out of illicit sales of alcohol. She half expected the likes of
Al Capone and Bugs Moran to be waiting for her with

machine guns at the ready. But nobody seemed interested in drilling her full of lead. Animates were swilling whiskey, embracing at tables, jigging the Charleston. The men were in dinner suits, the women in short, straight, flapper-style dresses hung with beads and with flowers in their bobbed hair. Nobody seemed interested in her at all.

Except the waiter, courteously appearing at her elbow. 'Good evening, Miss,' he said smoothly. 'May I offer you something?'

Lori was about to refuse – the consumption of alcohol during missions was not conducive to survival – until she glanced down at the silver tray the waiter was wafting under her nose. There was no bottle or glass upon it, instead a Judson 1927 submachine gun rendered in black, nicknamed the Reaper.

'I'll take it,' said Lori.

'And if I may also relieve you of these?' Her western weapons. 'You'll no longer be requiring them, Miss.'

There still appeared no immediate requirement for a firearm of any description. The speakeasy's clientele seemed unconcerned that the new arrival should be toting a machine gun. The music played. The dancers danced. The drinkers drank.

If they all suddenly turned hostile, she'd have no chance.

What was Judson up to? Toying with her? Well, he'd find out that Lori Angel wasn't to be toyed with. Across the crowded club was the main entrance, attained by a short flight of stairs with a man waiting to take hats and coats standing by the door. On the other side, the third gallery.

Lori had no choice. With the Judson Reaper pointed

ahead of her, she ventured into the body of the club. 'Excuse me. Excuse me.' Stepping cautiously among the tables. Speaking politely to animates evidently programmed to ignore her. Maybe something had gone wrong with this gallery. Maybe Wolf had changed his mind. Her muscles tautened with tension.

There was a smash and a scream to her right.

Lori whirled, on the brink of opening fire. A flapper had knocked a bottle of champagne to the floor. *It* had exploded. *She* had squealed. False alarm.

Lori attempted to breathe a sigh of relief.

Then the door burst open and the fun began.

Men in fedoras and long black coats. Men armed with submachine guns. Men who meant business. Gangsters. Half a dozen of them, each one raking the floor of the speakeasy with bullets.

Whether the waiter at the door would have asked them for their exterior garments was a moot point. He was the first to die, propelled backwards by the force of fire, crashing through the banister and thudding on to a table spilling drinks in the laps of the revellers. They didn't have time to protest before the machine guns ripped through them and ruined their clothes more permanently than a splash of cocktail.

There was panic in the speakeasy as its denizens dived for cover, as its dancers jerked to a fatal tune – the staccato rattle of the guns.

At least Lori didn't have to concern herself about casualties. The only real human here was her, and as she dived for cover behind an upended table, she knew that somehow she had to get *past* the sextet of gangsters to the door.

She edged out beyond the rim of the table, signalled her intent with a burst of gunfire. Her Reaper knew its job. A gangster followed the flight path of the hat and coat man. But now his companions knew where she was and combined their firepower, blizzarded her with bullets. Lori flinched back. That was *too* close, and the admittedly sturdy oak of her table shield couldn't resist the machine gun assault for long.

The speakeasy's animate clientele were either dead or fled by now. Neither was an option that could be contemplated by Angel Blue.

A quick rattle of her Reaper and then she retreated behind cover again. Her isolated resistance was not affecting the mobsters' tactics. They weren't being lured to finish her off, making themselves easier targets the closer they came. Instead they were strung out on the stairs, all five of them in a row, taking advantage of the height to shoot down on Lori.

All her training had taught her to aim for the torso first, the largest solid area, the likeliest to hit.

Training wasn't always right.

Lori rolled out from behind the splintering table, sprayed the staircase with bullets. Aimed low. Aimed between the wooden uprights that supported the handrail. Aimed for legs.

If Wolf Judson hadn't realised it already, he soon would. Lori was a very good shot.

One by one the gangsters tipped and reeled, lost the power to stand. Lori used hers. She was up and running, vaulting the bodies of the fallen animates, still maintaining an unbroken stream of gunfire. Her targets writhed and juddered as they collapsed, tried to haul themselves up again, tried to continue with their program.

Lori stood at the bottom of the stairs, and the clatter of her Reaper made that impossible. Black coats shredded. Fedoras crumpled and dislodged. Eyes stared blindly.

Lori snapped off her weapon. There was silence in the speakeasy. 'You dirty rats,' she couldn't resist drawling. She thought she deserved a moment of levity. Only a moment, however.

Their were still two more galleries to go.

'Is it me, or is Lori doing pretty well?' mused Casino as the blonde girl moved on. He looked from the monitor screen to Wolf Judson enthroned alongside him. 'You fancy a little wager on how long it'll take her to get here, Mr Judson, sir?'

Wolf Judson glanced at Casino. 'A task half-finished is a task not finished at all, my young friend. I wouldn't permit Lori's early successes to raise your hopes of rescue.'

'No?' Casino did not shrink from Judson's stare.

'No. Neither should you expect assistance from any other source – Ms Angel's colleagues, for example. The same intelligence that led my men to you has also led to them. You are alone, boy.' Wolf snorted. 'As alone as the dead you are soon to join.'

'Well, I'd help myself,' Casino said, 'but I'm a bit tied up at the moment.'

Wolf chuckled, returned his attention to the screen.

Which was just the way Cas liked it. His wrists were bound now, yes, but not, he hoped, for much longer. Behind his back he was rubbing them together, creating friction, flexing and unflexing his fists and the muscles of his forearms, creating slack. He'd been doing this since Wolf's men had first lashed him to the throne. He hadn't paused for a second and he wasn't going to now.

Not even as 1920s Chicago became 1940s Europe, and Nazis replaced gangsters as Lori's animate opponents. War-torn city streets, trembling as the bombs dropped in the distance, the buildings already roofless and crumbling. Cas saw Lori, her Reaper swapped for a regulation US Army M-3 .45 calibre submachine gun. 'Manufactured by us, of course,' Wolf was explaining, his words barely registering. 'My great-grandfather called it the Judson Jerry-picker, one of our little contributions to the war effort.' The Jerry-picker was going to have to make more than a *little* contribution, Cas feared, if Lori was going to make it through the German gun emplacement that was presently pinning her down. The stormtroopers had sandbagged themselves a virtually impregnable position in front of the scarred shell of a building within which could be clearly glimpsed the door to the fourth gallery. Firing low wouldn't help her this time.

Cas gazed enviously at the control panel set into the throne-arm that Wolf was using to operate the scenarios. If he was free, if he could deactivate this whole museum murder machine, then Lori wouldn't have to worry about Nazis, gangsters or anybody else. He kept working his wrists. It was a trick he'd learned from an old escapologist friend of his father's, back in those distant days when he'd had a father and his father had had friends.

Lori was exchanging fire but making no progress.

Wolf was chuckling as if he expected it all to be over imminently.

Marvellous Mervyn, the guy was called, the Heir to Houdini. No bonds could bind him nor ropes restrain, that was his boast. In those days it was enough to earn him a modest living in the cheaper shows on the fringes of Vegas, the income at least more regular than Cas's father's gambling. Mervyn had shown little Robbie how you could get out of any knot by bunching your muscles before it was tied and then by generating friction with your wrists. You needed sweat. Sweat was the key. For Casino, possibly minutes from death, sweat was not a problem.

A problem was Lori. Had she gone mad? Had her mind snapped under the strain? What was she doing firing wildly into the air, high above the Germans' heads, hitting only the wall behind them?

Quicker. He needed to be quicker. It had been generous of Marvellous Mervyn to share his secrets all those years ago, but the secrets themselves hadn't actually done the escapologist much good. He'd drowned soon afterwards, not *quite* surfacing from the bottom of a tank of water in time. When they'd drained it, they'd found his wrists still tied to a two-ton weight.

Cas was experiencing something of that sinking feeling himself.

Or maybe not. It was his turn to chuckle. He should never have doubted Lori, not for a second. She was irresistible – and in more ways than one.

She hadn't been firing wildly. She'd been thinking laterally. You didn't have to shoot your enemies to eliminate them. An already tottering concrete wall dumped on their heads would do the job just as well. Thanks to the added encouragement of a sustained assault from Lori's Jerry-picker, that was exactly what had happened. The German gun emplacement was a threat no longer.

'I've heard of bringing the roof down, but that's ridiculous,' Casino quipped.

Wolf glared.

Casino thought he'd better keep working on his bonds.

And the fourth gallery wasn't going to stop her, either. She was on more familiar territory here: the food riots during the Great Contamination of the 2020s; she was more comfortable with her weapon, a pacifier blaster used for crowd control. It was tempting to let her mind drift to the inevitable confrontation with Judson.

Tempting, but unacceptable. In the field, nothing was inevitable. Not death. Not victory. As with all aspects of life, what happened was what you *made* happen.

Which meant she needed to shoot the riot police out of the sky.

The street was broad but it seemed narrow, clogged with marchers and protestors. The riot police were seeking to disperse the gathering from the vantage point of SkyBikes. They were doing so violently. They were shooting to kill, and their main focus for termination was Lori.

As they swooped, she fired back, unseating them, plummeting them to earth. The riderless SkyBikes crashed into the crowd, scattering or disabling the animates. But while some still remained operational and in role, obeying their protestor programming, Lori could use them as mechanical shields. And she'd learned how to play the galleries now. Her marksmanship was lethal and economical.

At the end of the street was a police precinct building. Its door was *her* door.

It was defended by a Public Disturbance Control Platform. A hovering metal disc, of a diameter wide enough to accommodate twelve riot police at evenly spaced intervals around its circumference, each man armoured and protected within a revolving turret that bristled with weaponry. Big guns and lots of them. It made Lori feel almost inadequate.

The PDCP glided slowly in her direction. Its operator, the thirteenth member of its crew ensconced in a glasteel bubble at the hub of the platform, obviously doubted that time was of the essence. A single foe, however adept, had little chance against a fully functioning PDCP.

The remaining rioting animates fled as the street erupted towards them. Lori was left behind.

She stood her ground.

The pacifier, like the shock blasters she more commonly employed, contained a setting for Materials, providing shells with greater explosive impact. She switched to that. She had the opportunity for one shot before the platform ended her tenure as an agent of the Deveraux organisation, before Somebody-Else Blue took over.

Before she let Casino down. And Shades. And Jake. And . . .

She fired, both hands on the blaster. The operator's glasteel bubble smithereened in an instant, whooshed into flame.

The platform's directional and height controls went haywire.

By the time it crashed into the street, ploughing a furrow through the gallery's maintenance systems, Lori had reached the fourth door, the final door.

If he hadn't been lying, the next person she saw would be Wolf Judson.

He hadn't been lying. There was a short, dark corridor. Then there was another door.

Then there was Wolf.

Lori emerged into the chamber with the throne, Wolf lounging in it as if he had no worries at all, Casino bound beside it, getting to his feet hopefully as he saw her.

'Are you okay, Cas?' she called, her eyes lighting on another door beyond the throne – potential escape route?

'I am now.' Though still working at the ropes. His right hand was all but free.

'Hi, Wolf. You know something? The style of your hospitality is really starting to get on my nerves. What say we save time now and just cut to the Chase. Your brother Chase. Where is he, Wolf? Where are he and Stockdale and the others? Just what are you up to?'

If Wolf Judson was in any way surprised by Lori's words, he did not reveal it. He did not move. 'You may as well put that pacifier down, Lori. Outside the museum it is quite useless. Besides, as you can see, I am unarmed myself.' He raised his arms to prove the point.

'My mother told me never to trust men with pony-tails,' Lori retorted. 'Maybe you're lying about the gun.' He had to have a contingency plan, otherwise surely the chamber would be packed with his black-suited lackeys.

'Try it, my dear,' invited Wolf. 'Fire it and see.'

'All right, I will.' Lori shot harmlessly at the wall. *Extremely* harmlessly. She pulled the trigger but no shell was discharged. The firing mechanism had somehow been deactivated.

'There you are,' smiled Wolf craftily. 'As I told you, quite useless. An effective weapon in its day, however. My father couldn't manufacture them fast enough back in the 2020s. But every firearm eventually becomes obsolete. The key to success in my business is to anticipate the market in advance, to predict trends and to be ready for them. To constantly apply the latest technology to the science of killing.'

'I'm not here for the sales pitch, Judson,' warned Lori.

Wolf Judson stood. He was powerful, regal, intimidating.

'He's up to something!' Casino called, struggling to shift the rope over his knuckles.

'Consider, for example, our most recent innovation.' Lori braced herself warily, uncertain how to respond to Wolf's unexpected behaviour. 'In these lawless times, personal security is an ever more pressing priority, and who wants to have to rely on a handgun from which you can be so easily parted?' What was he talking about? 'Better, perhaps, to be protected by a weapon that is as much a part of you as your own body.'

The flesh of Wolf's left hand was quivering, bubbling, turning opaque.

'Gungrafts,' Wolf approved, pulling up his sleeve, baring his left forearm. Beneath the skin, it looked like maggots wriggling. 'The future of weapons technology.'

The flesh at Wolf's fingers split and retracted, slithered up his arm. Beneath it, glistening and oiled, was not muscle nor bone nor blood, but steel and circuitry. His fingers melted together and resolved themselves into the barrel of a gun.

'I'd like you to meet my firearm,' said Wolf.

TEN

'You can have one in any colour,' Wolf continued, gazing at the metal tube of his arm admiringly, almost lovingly, 'as long as it's silver. They're wired directly to the brain just like a human arm, operated by the owner's nerve impulses. A year's supply of special gungraft ammunition comes free with every model purchased.' Wolf's wild eyes gleamed as they seized on Lori. 'And they're guaranteed to kill all known enemies. Dead.'

'Lori!' Casino barged at Judson from the side. His prisoner's mobility still limited by the rope, Wolf had only to club him away with his human arm before returning his murderous attention to Lori. But Cas's intervention had still possibly saved her, given her a vital moment to recover from the shock of seeing the gungraft, allowed her to assimilate her situation. And *move*.

She leapt. Not at Wolf. That way was suicide. His left arm blazed from what had been his hand. Shells spat forth and riddled the floor where she'd been standing.

She leapt and she forward-rolled and she forward-rolled again, gunfire at her heels. How quickly could she move? How could she evade him?

Wolf stepped down from the throne. He was savouring the moment. And he was aware of the doors.

'No no no, Ms Angel.' Bursts of bullets cut her off from first one possible exit, then the other. 'You want to leave so soon? Whatever for? Aren't you having fun?'

I'll give you *fun*, beardie boy, vowed Casino inwardly. His teeth clenched. His heart hammered. His right hand was free. Just give me a second longer, he prayed.

Lori's legs had been filleted of muscle. It was as though she was in a movie that was being dragged into slow motion. Her gorge was rising. The museum galleries, they'd taken more out of her than she'd thought. She couldn't go on, but the firearm's ammunition seemed inexhaustible.

And then she was sprawling on the floor and the room was swaying sickly round her, and over her stood Wolf Judson with his gungraft smoking.

'A little tired, are we, my dear?' The feral teeth flashed. 'Then perhaps I'd better put you to sleep.'

'Go ahead,' Lori goaded. 'Kill me. If you're waiting for me to beg or start blubbering you can forget it. I haven't been trained that way. And neither have the other agents who'll come after you, who'll come after you and *get* you, Judson.'

'Ah.' Wolf was amused. '*Other* agents. I'm afraid they'll have just as little luck as you, my dear, and probably won't look as fetching in a bikini. Besides, I've already dealt with your colleagues in Las Vegas.'

'What?' She couldn't disguise the shock. Shades. Jake.

'Yes, Lori.' Judson saw it and feasted like a beast on red meat. 'I should be hearing confirmation . . .'

An alarm. Fittingly, like a lone wolf howling to the moon. Now it was Judson's turn to let the mask slip. 'Security alert,' he growled. 'It seems I presumed too much.'

'What did I tell you?' jeered Lori. 'They're going to take you down.'

'*They* might, conceivably,' said Wolf. '*You*, however —'

'Lori!' Casino's left hand was free. He launched himself at Judson.

Who heard him. Wheeled. Fired.

'Cas!' Lori's kick swept Judson's legs from under him. His firearm flailed. A little, but not enough. She saw the blood crimson Casino's side, saw him fall to the floor and cry out in pain. She struck at the small of Wolf's back. Strength was returning to her limbs, from where she didn't know and didn't care. It only mattered that she didn't falter, didn't fail, that she didn't give up.

Wolf lashed out with his firearm. It cracked against her temple, splitting the skin. He was struggling to his feet, preparing to shoot. She was rolling on the ground again as the shells sparked and scorched.

And then Wolf was running. With an audible curse he was leaving her and making for the door. He obviously dared to loiter no longer. The alarm was insistent. His priority was escape.

Hers ought to be to prevent that escape. It ought to be pursuit.

Instead she knelt by Casino. 'Cas, let me see . . .' He was clutching at his wounded side and his hand was red. He needed immediate attention. 'We need to get you —'

'No!' Casino refused through his hurt. 'You need to get *Judson*, Lori. Do it. This is just a . . . scratch . . .'

'Casino, I can't . . .'

'You can, Lori. You *have* to!'

He was right. 'I'll be back for you,' she promised. 'I *will*.' And she was springing to her feet, chasing after the vanished figure of Wolf Judson.

'Take your time,' Casino groaned. 'I'm not going anywhere.'

One of Wolf's men half-heartedly tried to stop her. She rendered him both unconscious and shock blasterless. Wolf was up ahead of her. She flung herself to one side as her quarry's firearm blazed to deter her. But she could return fire now. The pursuit was far from over.

If Casino died, if Judson had killed him, then Lori would . . . She thought of Jake, and the rage in him as he pressed his gun against Mickey Lorenzo's forehead – the anger that had nearly consumed him. She wouldn't let Wolf twist her, corrupt her, no matter how terrible his crimes. If Casino died, if Casino lived, Wolf Judson would face justice just the same.

Lori would make sure of it.

The corridor was widening now. Doors like elevator doors swished open at its end. There was no elevator beyond, however. Instead, Lori caught a glimpse of a helicopter with a dark shaft above it, open to the sky. Wolf's escape route. Lori had to stop him making it through those doors but two guards in overalls were emerging from within and covering him, forcing her to pause. They were adequate shots. Lori was exceptional. It would take her two seconds to stun them.

In two seconds, Wolf Judson had bolted into the helicopter bay.

In the further four seconds it took Lori to reach the doors, they had closed.

Her deactivator had been in her belt. It would take longer for her to disable the lock by hand. It was time she didn't have.

The Judson residence rumbled. Its foundations shook. The sound reminded Lori of a landslide or a distant avalanche. The sound reminded Lori that Wolf's dwelling was largely jammed between two steep sections of canyon wall. Its owner wasn't taking any chances.

The floor beneath her feet trembled, vibrated.

Casino. Lori wheeled and sprinted back the way she'd come.

He'd hauled himself across the floor and up onto the throne. A smear of blood marked his progress. He heard Lori call his name like an echo. 'Just trying . . . to get comfortable . . .' And everything was blurring, softening, like memories of childhood. And was the floor tipping slightly now or was it him?

Then she was strong beside him and snaking his arm round her neck, heaving him to feet that were like a puppet's without the puppeteer to work them. 'Lean on me,' she said.

'Thought . . . you'd never ask.' A thin smile. 'Wolf?'

'Don't worry about Wolf. We've got to get out of here.'

If he wanted to know why, the boom of detonations too close for comfort provided ample reason. As did the house's consequent lurch forward. It was not usual to design floors at a forty-five degree angle.

'He's sabotaged the whole place.' Lori moved as

swiftly as she could. Casino was heavy, though, and her own strength was beginning to ebb once more. It was hard not to jar his wounded side. 'He's going to bring it down, send it crashing to the floor of the canyon.'

'He could have just . . . asked us to leave,' winced Casino.

Lori quickly considered their options. Up the sloping corridors and deeper into the rockface, the way Lori had pursued Wolf earlier, hope to find the route through to the section of the house that was sited safely above ground and far from the canyon's edge? Or slide downwards, towards the chasm. That option would be quicker and more certain – the explosions were from inland, the charges clearly placed in such a pattern as to dislodge the dwelling from its already precarious position.

Lori chose the latter. There was the thousand metre drop to the Colorado River, true, but there was also the clingskin on her gloves and boots that would help her bear Casino down the canyon wall to her SkyBike and its emergency medical kit.

The remainder of Judson's men evidently thought otherwise. Several fled past Lori and Cas, scarcely registering their presence, it seemed, let alone attempting to apprehend them. 'Rats leaving the sinking ship,' muttered Lori.

'In a democracy,' Casino struggled, 'shouldn't we follow . . . the majority?'

'Let's make a stand for the individual's right to go his own way,' said Lori, 'or hers. Besides –' and she surged on with Casino more quickly still despite his cry of sudden, shooting pain – 'wherever they *think* they're heading, they won't make it in time.'

The house itself seemed to be groaning now, in an agonised voice of cracking, crunching rock. There was no need for further explosive encouragement, Wolf's charges had done their work. The distribution of the building's weight was now such that the tearing of itself away from the canyon, like a tumour scoured from healthy tissue, was inevitable.

And with a grating, grinding, rending roar, it began.

Lori and Casino stumbled into a room that gave out on to the upper terrace. For once it was fully furnished, and could have been stylish before it had dipped alarmingly downwards and hurled its contents at the glasteel doors. Being glasteel, of course they hadn't broken. Unfortunately, because if Lori had to deactivate the locks manually, their escape would be dangerously delayed. But the house's death-throes seemed to have disrupted its computer system. The doors' locks were already disengaged.

'Nearly there, Cas,' Lori rallied. 'Hold on.'

'Like I'm gonna let go?'

The entire structure was wobbling now, like a loose tooth about to be pulled. Lori had to lean back to keep her balance as they exited to the terrace itself. It was probably a good thing that it was pitch black: the view from here, almost vertical, to the canyon floor would not have been inspiring.

The building jerked forward, wavered, shook.

If not for the clingskin, Lori and Cas might have fallen by now. The terrace began to split along the middle, keen to shake them off.

And then Lori heard the rotors of a helicopter. Was Wolf too impatient to let gravity do his dirty work for him?

'Quickly, Cas,' Lori commanded. 'Behind me. Arms around my neck.'

'Lori, I can't . . .'

'Your words, Casino. You can. You *have* to!'

The black hulk of a helicopter rose from the canyon below them. The white glare of its spotlight pinned them to the terrace like bugs in a book.

'Wolf,' dreaded Lori.

'We're gonna train a tractor beam on you,' came a metallic voice over the chopper's loud-speaker. 'Try and keep relaxed. I know it won't be easy!'

Lori closed her eyes with relief. The voice was Jake's.

The very roots of the house tore loose. The twin terraces and the floors between, the museum galleries and the throne chamber and any of Wolf's men who'd not evacuated smartly enough, all crashed like a titanic exploding firework down the side of the Grand Canyon, scoring deep grooves and gashes in the rock that had survived the passage of a thousand centuries. A magnificent architectural achievement was reduced to rubble, smouldering on the canyon floor.

From the refuge of the chopper, Lori shed no tears. 'We could have been in there.'

'But you weren't,' Jake replied.

'No.' Lori turned to Casino, who was being attended by a medtech. Deveraux attack-helicopters came equipped with a small medilab including a bed At the present moment, its white coverall was stained red. 'Cas? Everything's going to be fine.' She squeezed his arm but he didn't respond, seemed barely conscious. She glanced anxiously at the medtech.

'He's lost a lot of blood,' the woman said. 'I've given him a sedative and we need to get him to hospital. But you were right, Agent Angel. He'll live.'

'Thank you.' A grateful sigh. The pricking of tears at the back of her eyes? 'Thank you. And thank *you*, Jake, too. If you hadn't appeared when you did, I'm not sure I would have had the strength to clingskin Cas down that canyon wall.'

'You would,' said Jake. 'You'd have found it from somewhere. You always do.'

She looked away from him, out at the desert and the night. The helicopter was returning to Las Vegas. A hospital room for Casino was already being prepared. And here was Jake being *nice* to her for the first time in a long time. How should she respond? Be business-like. 'You'd better brief me on what's been happening, Jake. Judson hinted that he'd sent men after you.'

'He did. They weren't very good. But Shades thought they gave us a legitimate reason to move in on Judson in force. One of them was persuaded to tell us they planned on abducting Casino and using him against you. Shades thought that under those circumstances you wouldn't be likely to refuse a little extra help.'

'As usual, Shades was right.' Lori grinned. It felt good. 'In fact, if you'd have come sooner it would have saved me a lot of trouble.' She recounted her recent experiences to Jake.

'What are you complaining about?' Jake teased. 'Little bit of a work-out. Good for you. Just a pity Judson got away.'

A momentary gloom settled on the two Spy High agents.

'For now, Jake,' said Lori. 'Only for now.'

'Maybe we should have attacked from the terraces instead, or as well, but it looked easier to gain a foothold by targeting the above-ground part of the house.' Jake shrugged. 'Guess we did that. We were forging ahead when the whole place started to rock and roll and we had to beat a retreat. I thought if you were still capable – and I knew you would be – you'd try to make it out canyon-side.'

'You know me so well, Jake.'

'Not as well as I used to.' He seemed to be closer to her now, as they sat propped in the helicopter's main cabin and the Nevada night swept by outside. 'Lori, there are things I need to say . . .'

She looked across to the sleeping form of Casino Royal. Twice now he'd risked his life to save hers. Not bad for a small-time hustler from the streets of Vegas. She remembered their first meeting, the broken vase for a probably non-existent Aunt Mildred. The memory made her smile. She'd have to ask Cas about that when he came round. She'd have to ask him about a lot of things.

Jake saw her look, saw her smile, knew what it meant. If he followed suit, his was thin and resigned.

'What, Jake? What did you need to say?' Maybe she'd imagined it before. Jake wasn't closer. If anything, he was further away.

'Yeah,' he said. 'About the mission.' Business-like. 'Soon as we gained entry to Judson's house we had a tech on the first computer we saw. The alarm must have triggered a virus in the system, though. Wolf's files were virtually all corrupted before the tech could do anything to save them.'

'*Virtually* all?'

'Yeah. One or two scraps of intelligence might prove useful – names of files.'

'Names?' Lori was intrigued.

'It seems you might have misheard Macey's final word,' said Jake, 'according to what the tech found. It looks like it might have been words rather than one word.'

'I don't understand.'

'We saved one of Wolf's most secret files. Not assassination, Lori. Assassin *nation*.'

ELEVEN

Hospitals and Lori Angel didn't mix. She could number her positive experiences of them on the thumbs of one hand.

Hopefully, today's visit to Casino would be an exception.

He looked better, certainly. He was sat up in bed in a very charming white hospital singlet, the spikiness had been combed out of his hair and his eyes were twinkling again.

'Hi,' she said at the door to his room. 'How are you feeling, Cas?'

'For someone who's been chased by guards, nearly torn to pieces by savage animates, humiliated by having to brave the streets of Vegas practically naked, kidnapped and then shot by a guy with a machine gun for an arm, and all in the last three days, I'm feeling pretty cool, thanks.'

Lori deduced from Casino's comically outraged tone that he was hamming. 'Keep ranting like that, Cas, and you'll have high blood pressure to add to the list.'

'It's the people I'm being forced to hang around with these days, Nurse Angel,' bemoaned Casino. 'They're a bad influence. They're leading me astray.'

'I guess I could always leave . . .'

'I'm not sure that'll be necessary, Nurse Angel.' His mood became a little more serious. 'Wolf missed all the major organs. But if it wasn't for you dragging me all the way out of there, I'd have been food for the coyotes. I owe you *big-time*, Lori Angel.'

Lori shook her head. 'If you hadn't drawn Wolf's attention away from me – risked sacrificing yourself – well, I doubt he'd have missed *my* major organs. The thanks are all mine.'

Casino smiled. 'Mutual gratitude society, huh?' They were both silent for a moment. 'So, you want to sit with the invalid and watch some videvision for a while?'

'I can't,' Lori admitted reluctantly. 'I just popped in to check . . . to see you . . . I've got to fly back East pretty much immediately. I have to report to my superiors, brief them.'

'Pity.' Cas suddenly found the top sheet of his bed highly interesting. 'Is, ah, is Jake going with you?'

'No. Jake's got his own assignment to return to,' Lori said. 'In fact, he's already left. Why?' Lori fished. 'Would Jake coming with me have bothered you?'

'No, no. It would have just been some company on the flight for you, that's all.' Casino thought it best to avoid mention of the slight altercation that had taken place between himself and Jake Daly. Hard Man had obviously thought the same. 'But when you get back, to your headquarters or base or centre of operations or whatever it is you call it, you'll be talking Wolf Judson, right? I know he escaped. The guard your organisation put on my door told me.'

'His name's likely to come up, yes.'

'And you'll be deciding on your next move, right? To *get* him, I mean.'

'I expect so.' Lori frowned. 'Cas, where are you going with this?'

'So you'll be throwing yourself right back into the thick of it. Espionage. Death-traps. Shoot-outs. Life on the line. Again. And no doubt again after that.'

'Sounds like you disapprove.'

'I haven't told you about my dad, have I, Lori?' Casino said. 'I guess we haven't had a chance yet to exchange anecdotes from our shady pasts. My dad, and I use the term biologically and not really in any other way, he was a gambler. A professional. He went all over the country when he was young and good at it, earning big money on the tables, at poker games and the races. He ended up in Vegas when he was older and not so good at it – when I was a kid. One of the very few nuggets of worthwhile advice he gave me – he only gave me advice when he was sober, so it wasn't often – was that the successful gambler was the gambler who knew when to stop, when *not* to take that final chance, when to get out with his winnings while the getting was good. The bad gambler, he said, was the guy who kept on playing, kept on taking risks, kept on pushing his luck. Because sooner or later that luck would run out, and then the gambler would destroy himself. My dad never took his own advice, of course, which is one reason why he's no longer with us.'

'Casino, I'm sorry . . .'

'I'm not sharing this for sympathy, Lori,' Casino claimed earnestly. 'I'm trying to *warn* you. 'Cause it may not seem like it to you, but I see a lot of similarities between a gambler's life and your kind of life – the secret agent stuff. Twice Wolf's had you and twice you've got away, each time by the skin of your pearly whites. A sensible gambler, if that's not a contradiction in terms, would call it a night and walk away, let somebody else see the table. You're not going to do that, though, are you? You're gonna roll the dice again, risk your life again. It's not worth it, Lori. Third time lucky. Third time unlucky. Don't take the chance.'

Lori regarded Casino with dismay. 'I thought you understood, Cas. What I do isn't about risk, it's about responsibility. Mine. To be the best person I can be. To do something I can be proud of. To make a difference. I thought because you stayed at the motel you'd decided to —'

'No, Lori,' Cas interrupted. 'Judson's men didn't catch me at the motel. I'd left. I was going . . . I don't know where I was going. Somewhere. Nowhere. Running away, I guess you'd call it.'

'I see.' Lori's expression was bleak. 'Anyway, I can't sit and . . . I just popped in to check . . . how you were doing. I think I know now.' Suddenly there was awkwardness in the room. The conversation had taken a course neither of them had expected – nor enjoyed. Lori stood. 'Cas, I know you've got to stay in here for five days' further observation. If I came back before then, would you still want to see me?'

'Maybe you should turn the question around, Lori,'

said Casino. 'Once you've been back with your secret agent friends, would you still want to see *me*?'

'Take care of yourself, Cas,' said Lori.

The President of the United States out jogging was usually a valuable photo-opportunity. It showed a man of middle age and gracefully greying hair unafraid to expose his legs for the nation's newspapers and vide-vision channels (said limbs having discreetly undergone a little physical reconstruction to create just the right visual impression, muscles resculpted and stained with non-fading tanning agent, like wood). It revealed a man aware of the necessity for a healthy lifestyle and pre-pared to push, push, push himself, for the benefit of the country as well as his respiratory system. Usually, Graveney Westwood's press secretary would have the photographers lined up to snap the great man as he pounded the streets in his 'All The Way USA' jogging shirt.

But there were two problems with that today. Firstly, the president had been jogging in the verdant and expan-sive grounds of Camp Lincoln, which nobody outside the country's political and security elite knew existed. Secondly, after speaking to FBI Director Quilby, the jog had degenerated somewhat into a frantic scramble for the compound, and pictures of the president in panic would have done nothing for his popularity ratings.

'Gayle? Gayle!' Westwood tore into his vice-presi-dent's office, ducking and dodging to avoid being seen at the window. 'Have you heard? Quilby's just told me about that ungrateful son of a Mississippi water-rat who they think's plotting against me.'

'I have been informed, Mr President, sir,' said Gayle Steinwitz coolly. Directly from Agent Carmody, as she'd instructed. 'Wolf Judson.'

'Wolf Judson? Wolf *Judson*? Is that all you can say, Gayle?' Westwood was incredulous that she could still be sitting calmly at her desk while he was pacing up and down in a sweat like a man on death row whose appeal had been denied ten minutes before his execution. 'D'you know what this *means*?'

'I'm sure our various security agencies have the situation well in hand, sir.'

'It means I'm in big trouble, Gayle, that's what it means,' Westwood wailed. 'Are you aware of how powerful the Judson family is, the kind of respect and I'd even go as far as to say *hero*-worship they receive from certain sections of this nation's fine community of patriotic and upstanding citizens? Do you know how many of their supporters own guns and know how to use 'em?' The president paused. 'Neither do I, but I'm telling you, Gayle, it ain't a *few*. Why d'you think we did arms deals with Wolf, promoted his brother Chase way above his level of competence when he was alive? I kept the Judsons sweet as far as I could, and this is how Wolf repays me? I want the present levels of security at Lincoln doubled, Gayle, y'hear me? No, trebled. I want it done *now*. If not *sooner*. And I want Wolf Judson caught.'

'We have agents engaged in the search now, Mr President,' informed Gayle, 'for Wolf and, apparently, for his younger sister Diana as well.' A note of what might have been interest or surprise almost entered her voice. 'I can't imagine why.'

'I don't care about Diana Judson,' Westwood raved. 'I want Wolf. I want him found. I want him foiled. I want him in the strongest damn cell this great country of ours has got. And I want Debbie. Where's Debbie? She's never here when I need her. Gayle,' as he blundered out, 'I'm holding you responsible. D'you know what this *means*?'

Gayle Steinwitz waited for her superior to shout his way down the corridor before murmuring under her breath, 'Oh, I think so, Mr President.' And she waited until even a man with telescopic implants and in good light would not have been able to see it before she permitted her features to express the contempt she was feeling. Icebergs didn't always melt. Sometimes they simply cracked.

Gayle Steinwitz could not be patient for very much longer.

Jake's email was waiting for her when she arrived back at Spy High. It didn't do much to lift her mood. 'It was good to see you again, Lori. Good to be on the team again, even briefly. Like old times. But talking *new* times, I just hope you know what you're doing having Casino around. Not that I have any right to comment on your private life any more, *but* (I'm not going to let that stop me!) I'd be careful if I were you. I'm not sure how far this Casino guy can be relied upon, and this is not jealousy talking, in case you're wondering. I'm a friend who's concerned you don't set yourself up to get hurt, that's all.' There was more in the same vein, but Jake really needn't have bothered with any of it. Given the tone of their last parting, Casino was probably no longer a matter for concern. As for her former team-mate and boyfriend's other major point, it came a little late.

She was already hurt.

Her meeting with Ferns the technician deepened her gloom. Whenever agents returned to the Deveraux College, either between missions or, as now, during them, they were obliged to undertake a field technology refresher session, to update them on the latest gadgets and scientific innovations developed by the techs and on which their lives might one day depend.

Ferns was introducing her to what he called the Deveraux chip.

Lori could always gauge her relative temper by her response to the tech's famously gyrating head. She knew she was in good humour when its apparently unstoppable wavers and wobbles only served to amuse her; she knew she was feeling low when her reaction was, instead, one of irritation. Today she felt like either tearing the offending object entirely off the hapless Ferns' shoulders or ramming it so far down between them that there would be absolutely no chance of movement and that he'd be speaking from just below his collar bone.

She needed to concentrate, though – forget Ferns, and Jake, and Casino . . . Focus on what the tech was saying about the Deveraux chip. He held one in his hand for Lori to see, but then, one computer chip looked very much like another. It was a tiny gleam in the centre of his palm.

'It's really an extension of the technology you used to defeat Dr Frankenstein aboard the Guardian Star while you were still a student here, Agent Angel,' Ferns was explaining.

Lori remembered the incident well. It had been during their mission to prevent the geneticist descendent of Victor Frankenstein from unleashing the Guardian Star space station's firepower on Earth that she and the rest of Bond Team had first met the president. Indeed, the fact that vast tracts of land still burgeoned with cities or flourished with forest and were not now reduced to scorched and radioactive ruin was thanks to her team's eventual success. And *that* had only been achieved, Lori mused, thanks to a computer chip implanted in her teammate Bex's brain, one that had allowed Jonathan Deveraux himself to board the Guardian Star and to override its weapons systems with his irresistible computer mind.

And now the Deveraux chip that Ferns was showing her was going to perform the same function? Make Jonathan Deveraux, the founder of Spy High, mobile?

'Not exactly, Agent Angel,' said Ferns, his head perched as precariously on his neck as Humpty Dumpty on his wall. 'These devices will not have direct access to Mr Deveraux's cyber-consciousness, at least not yet. What they will contain is a program, predetermined by us, providing behavioural instructions for the host body.'

'The host body?' The term sounded disturbingly clinical to Lori.

'Yes.' Ferns's head bobbed to the left, searching for something on the table of instruments in front of him. Like a surgeon's instruments before an operation, Lori thought. 'Ah, there you are.' He selected a syringe of a type, very small, slim, opaque, but already filled with a viscous grey liquid. 'The Deveraux chip, you see, Agent

Angel, is useless to us unless and until injected into the brain of a host.'

'You mean with that?' Lori's lips curled squeamishly as she indicated the syringe. 'That's not nice.'

'Nice?' Ferns seemed not to understand the word. 'Mr Deveraux wants technology developed for its efficiency in achieving our aims, not for its possible aesthetic value,' he said, his head nodding its agreement. 'And if I may assure you, Agent Angel, the Devereaux chip is most efficient.'

'I'm sure it is, Ferns,' said Lori, but not with enthusiasm.

'The cranial syringe, you will note,' continued the tech, 'contains, as you might expect, cranial fluid. Before deployment in the field, it will also contain a Deveraux chip with a program relevant and appropriate for the furtherance of the specific mission. The agent will locate a suitable host, incapacitate it –' *It?* pondered Lori – 'and inject it with the chip, placing the syringe against the fleshy part of the temple like so.' Ferns demonstrated.

'Careful,' Lori winced.

Luckily, Ferns's fingers were steadier than his head, and they were not tempted to accidentally depress the syringe. 'The Deveraux chip will attach itself to the frontal lobe of the host's brain and assume immediate control of its neural functions. From that moment on, the host will be incapable of independent thought or action until the chip is removed. It will be *entirely* in the thrall of our programming. Instead of an enemy, we will have an ally.'

'And instead of a human being,' Lori commented with a frown, 'a mindless zombie.'

Ferns did not detect the criticism implied by Lori's tone, probably because he was so utterly captivated by the computer chip itself, holding it up to the light and gazing admiringly at it like a jeweller examining a diamond. 'Mr Deveraux is a genius,' Ferns sighed. 'The potential of the Deveraux chip in combating and nullifying the threat of aberrant social behaviour in the future is truly awesome.'

Yeah, right, thought Lori. That was the solution to people who did bad things. Stick a computer chip in their heads so they were physically capable of nothing but good. Only, what about free will and the value of choice? If you removed from a human being their responsibility for their own actions and for the consequences of those actions, didn't you also remove from them a vital ingredient of what it was to be human in the first place? Yeah, and who was going to decide what was deemed *good* and what was not? Who would program the programmers?

All issues that Lori felt she'd like to discuss with Mr Deveraux at some point if she had time. It turned out she didn't. Barely had she finished her refresher session with Ferns than she was summoned to Briefing Room One. Shades was already there. So, on a screen, was the iron-grey, austere visage of Jonathan Deveraux.

'Be seated, Angel Blue,' invited the founder. 'We have fresh intelligence concerning the Judson assignment.'

The precise meaning of the phrase 'assassin nation', it seemed, remained elusive, but its sense was not as cryptic as before. 'Unfortunately, as you know,' said Jonathan Deveraux, 'we were unable to capture Wolf Judson or any of his men alive. Fortunately, however, not all of the latter escaped. And, thanks to our forensic scientists and techniques, even the dead can speak. Several bodies were recovered from the wreckage of Judson's house. Some were too crushed or mangled to be of use to us, but others were tolerably whole and could be examined. Beneath the deceased's fingernails, hiding in their pores, sometimes clinging secretly to the fabric of their clothing or the tread of their boots, we found evidence of a place far from here. Specks of soil, traces of grasses and plants that were discovered, after chemical analysis, not to be indigenous to the United States but native to certain islands in the Pacific Ocean, in international waters off the coast of Chile.'

Nobody ever escaped Jonathan Deveraux, Lori thought, nobody and nothing. He was alert to every detail of every mission undertaken by the agents of Spy High. He was as infallible as . . . well, as a computer. She was glad he was on their side.

'Our satellites scanned the islands in question,' the founder continued, 'and detected a significant anomaly on the land mass known as St Dominguez.'

The smart-desk on either side of which Lori and Luanne Carmody were seated now generated a three-dimensional representation of what Lori assumed to be the island of St Dominguez. It lacked any geographical features, being almost entirely flat and without major rivers. Jungle fringed its beaches before declining into scrubland at its centre, like the tonsure of a monk. The only man-made constructions that Lori could make out were a cluster of stone and wooden buildings in a cleared area of jungle close to a bay, and though the scale of the hologram challenged her eyesight, she thought that even these appeared old, ruined and abandoned.

'St Dominguez was once a slave colony owned by the Spanish,' informed Jonathan Deveraux. 'The remains of the sugar plantation that the early settlers built are still visible. The lack of fresh water resources on the island, however, made its long-term habitation difficult and eventually untenable. By the middle of the eighteenth century, Spaniards and slaves had left. Few people have attempted to dwell on the island since. Its official population at present is zero. We think that to be a rather pessimistic estimate.'

'Is this the source of the anomaly, sir?' ventured Lori.

'It is, Angel Blue. Our satellite pictures *seem* to attest to a total absence of human occupation, but when examined more closely –' a sequence of aerial views of St Dominguez suddenly replaced the hulk of the island – 'it can be seen that what we have photographed is not real.'

Lori nodded. She could distinguish the shimmer in the image that had less to do with heat-haze than with holograms. 'It's a holographic shield, like the ones we use here of kids playing football and of students in the corridors to mask what *really* happens at Spy High.'

'I wonder what's *really* happening on St Dominguez,' said Shades.

'A most pertinent question, Field Handler Carmody,' accepted Jonathan Deveraux, 'and one to which we must seek immediate answers, particularly as it is logical to assume that whatever the island seems to have to hide, it will be connected to the Judson family. There is, however, a further obstacle to overcome.'

'Sir?' Lori thought of Wolf's gungraft spewing death

in her direction, of Casino's cry as his side was torn open. It was going to have to be an obstacle of colossal magnitude to deter her.

'Once our sensors went to work on St Dominguez,' enlightened Deveraux, 'they also detected the presence of an energy barrier cocooning the island, rendering a full-scale landing or assault impracticable. Therefore, we need an agent to go in alone and to deactivate the energy barrier. There is no telling in advance what might await her. Angel Blue?'

'Sir,' Lori said, 'when do I leave?'

TWELVE

The chameleon suit was out of the question, of course, now that Judson had successfully developed counter-technology to neutralise its camouflaging properties. Lori would have to complete her mission in more conventional khaki. She trusted that the other fruits of Deveraux genius, however – her sleepshot wristbands, her shock blaster and the contents of her regulation Spy High issue belt – would be sufficient to provide her with an edge if and when she needed it.

First, though, she had to pierce the energy barrier without announcing her arrival in a burst of flame like a secret agent firework. That meant using a stealth-sphere. The sphere's ability to infiltrate enemy defences undetected was not quite as advanced as that of a chameleon suit, but its nano-chip signature was different, owing to the plasteel material from which it was constructed. At least Lori would have a chance.

A tech helped her into her sphere as the Pacific Ocean blurred by thousands of feet below them. Lori did not require much assistance. She'd experienced space-spheres before, when boarding the Guardian Star, and stealth-spheres were of similar style and purpose: a transparent plasteel bubble, large enough to accommodate anyone shorter than Goliath standing upright inside. An entirely self-sustaining environment, with lighting when necessary, life support systems, everything. Stirrups for the feet, gauntlets for the hands, a harness for the upper body, just in case the stabilising mechanism failed or was damaged by enemy fire during its long descent to the ground. Or, in Lori's case, to the sea.

'St Dominguez air-space approaching,' the plane's pilot announced over a tannoy. 'ETA one minute.'

'Are you comfortable, Agent Angel?' asked the tech.

Lori grinned at him as she made final adjustments to her harness. 'I'm suspended from the inside of an aircraft in what's little more than a balloon with attitude above a hatch which in less than sixty seconds is going to open, sending me plunging thirty thousand feet into the Pacific Ocean by an island where who knows how many bad guys might be waiting to kill me. Of *course* I'm comfortable!'

'Then good luck, Agent Angel,' said the tech. 'I'm sealing the sphere.'

He did so and backed swiftly away. Lori was on her own. What spy wasn't, she thought. ('ETA thirty seconds.') In the end, however much you trusted your team-mates, and she'd trusted hers implicitly, time and again your continued survival came down to *you*, what *you* did, how *you* acted, how well *you'd* absorbed all they'd taught you at Spy High and beyond. In the end, survival was a matter of selfishness. ('ETA twenty seconds.') Maybe that was why she found it so hard to form and keep meaningful relationships with the opposite sex. ('Ten seconds.') Relationships were supposed to be about sharing, about compromise, while in the field you had to be just the opposite – ruthless, single-minded. ('Five.') It was a problem. Because just when you felt you wanted to work at a relationship, in her line of business there was never enough . . .

The hatch opened. The sphere dropped.

Lori plummeted towards the sea.

There was nothing she could do about the contents of her stomach suddenly seeming determined to gang together and force their way to freedom via her gullet. It was an inevitable physical response to a fall of such precipitous proportions. Not even a Deveraux chip could have mastered it. Only willpower. The willpower that also steadied Lori's fear, her sense of dislocation from the world, of vulnerability. She was a ball hurled from the heavens, a speck spinning through vast and empty space. Fear and its manifestations, mental *or* physical, were indulgences that a Spy High operative could not allow herself. Emotions had to be subjugated, the mind directed to the mission.

The island rushed up to meet her, the holographic sheet pulled over it as if it were a sleeping child.

She plunged into the energy barrier, almost felt it crackle with power. It flared briefly as she passed through, but the stealth-sphere kept her alive, the plasteel smoking.

The island was visible again. Beneath the illusion of unoccupation she caught a glimpse of concrete and steel buildings of a style rather more recent than the eighteenth century.

Then Lori's sphere struck the surface of the ocean like one of those World War Two bouncing bombs she'd seen in old films, throwing up spumes of spray like solid debris. The sphere didn't bounce, though – it wasn't designed to. Instead, it began to sink. The stealth part of its name wouldn't be usefully served if it bobbed gently on the sea to be spotted by anyone with a pair of binoculars.

It began to sink, but that was fine. The interior lighting would come on automatically as the solar-sensitive plasteel shell detected darkness; the exit panel would hiss open; Lori would simply vacate the sphere and swim to the island.

Or not.

No lights came on. No panel hissed open. And Lori's unexpectedly wet feet proved that water was seeping into the bottom of the sphere.

The energy barrier must have damaged the craft's systems. Lori frowned. An agent in the field was allowed to frown as long as that was not her only reaction to adversity. She unclasped her hands from their gauntlets, unbuckled her harness. If she couldn't get out of here the easy way, she'd have to take the *hard* way. She tried to release her feet from their stirrups. Her left foot came away; her right foot did not. The stirrup mechanism was jammed.

The sphere was sinking and the water was over her ankles.

Now her frown deepened, was supplemented by a choice word or two that would not have featured in any secret agent handbook. Contingency measures: Lori squatted in the cold water, tried to force the stirrup open with her fingers. No good. The deactivator from her belt? The locking mechanism, however damaged, might still be overridden.

The ocean outside was deeper now and darker, the invading water reaching her waist.

No good.

She had her belt-breather, of course, a guarantor of ten minutes' worth of oxygen. Trouble was, if she didn't get out soon, she'd have need of some of that to reach the surface again.

The sphere was flooding more quickly now, as if the ocean was keen to drown her while it had the chance. More drastic measures were required.

Lori drew her shock blaster.

She daren't try 'Materials': that might well shatter the stirrup, but it would do the same to the foot inside. She had to hope that a routine stun blast, aimed precisely at the locking mechanism, would be sufficient to snap it open.

With water now at her neck, Lori did not hesitate. She gulped a breath, ducked under, pressed the blaster's nozzle against the offending lock. Pressed the trigger. A jolt of agony seared through her foot, numbing, crippling. If opening her mouth to scream had not been inviting instant death, Lori would have done it. But pain, like fear, could be mastered by willpower.

And her foot was free.

But the sphere was flooded. Lori paused only to take her belt-breather from its pouch at her waist and fit it into her mouth, like a boxer's gum-shield. Then she *did* set the shock blaster to 'Materials'. Pressed her back against one curved side of the bubble. Fired at the other.

Stealth-spheres were made of sturdy material. Cracks and fissures in the plasteel appeared, like the sudden web of an aquatic spider, but no means of escape. Lori fired again.

This time the sphere burst like an egg dropped to the floor.

Lori kicked off and swam towards the surface. The pain in her right foot was already diminishing to a dull ache. A minor delay, perhaps, but her mission was now back on track.

And maybe her luck was changing. No bad guys were waiting for her in boats and wielding weapons trademarked Judson. She could swim unmolested to St Dominguez, though she kept underwater as far as possible just in case. There was no apparent guard or look-out on the beach, either. Wolf – if Wolf was here – seemed to be investing a lot of trust in the hologram and the energy barrier. To rely on technology alone was always careless.

Lori waded ashore like a well-armed Robinson Crusoe.

She'd been dropped off the coast of the island nearest to the old slave plantation. The mission planners thought she might be able to use it as a base if necessary, as additional cover. Her task now was to reach it.

Lori raced up the beach – too open, too dangerous – and into the cover of the jungle. She stole swiftly through its tangled pathways and dappled light. Her khaki camouflage suit was already almost dry. Her foot was suffering only the memory of pain. She was feeling good, confident, tuned in. This was what she'd trained for. This was what made her feel alive. If Casino couldn't or wouldn't understand that, then maybe they *didn't* have any kind of future, maybe a relationship with him simply *wasn't* possible.

Then she came to the graveyard. If it could be called that. A humble scrap of land once cleared by men but now almost totally reclaimed by the jungle. Yet the graves were still here, marked by cracked and splitting wooden crosses, the anonymous graves of illiterate slaves. The plot had been too small to show up on the holographic rendition of St Dominguez that Deveraux had shown her, just as the dead men and women buried here had been deemed too inconsequential to be marked on the map of history. But they had lived, and they had been victims of one form of injustice on this remote and undistinguished isle. Now another kind of evil was stirring here, Lori was sure of it, and while she could do nothing about the past, influencing the present was still within her power.

A sobering reminder for Angel Blue. It wasn't about feeling good or confident or tuned in. It was about doing the right thing, whatever the consequences.

The hollows of the plantation buildings were just ahead. Lori absorbed the layout as a matter of course. Twin rows of roofless wooden huts, some of the walls sagging, like sentries left too long on duty – the old slave quarters. The timber skeletons of the barns where the raw sugar-cane was once stored and processed.

Lori pushed on. This was a possible refuge, but her primary focus was ahead of her still: the buildings she'd seen in the centre of St Dominguez. There was only a final swathe of jungle between herself and them.

And something more, it seemed. Maybe Wolf Judson wasn't so careless after all.

She heard their voices, sullen and complaining, heard the heavy tramp of booted feet. Lori became a shadow while she listened.

'. . . waste of time, this is. Lashman's seeing things. He's spent so long staring at screens he's got spots in front of his eyes. That's what he saw. A spot in front of his eyes.'

'You're right, mate. Nobody can get through the energy barrier. If we find anything, it'll be a charred corpse, and I don't even reckon —'

'I don't care what you "reckon", Max. Mr Judson doesn't care. If he says investigate, we investigate, right? And keep your moaning mouth *shut*.'

'Okay, Stockdale, keep your safety catch on. We can do our job.'

Nah, thought Lori. You *can't* do your job. What you need is a bit of a rest.

There were five of them, strung out in an advancing line some ten metres apart from each other, all wearing army fatigues and carrying pulse rifles. Dane Stockdale was at their centre. Even if he hadn't been identified by one of his companions, Lori would have recognised him. He looked good for a guy who'd already died twice. She was almost pleased to see him.

She could take them all if she wanted to. Wouldn't even need her shock blaster. But on the plus side, it made such a great noise.

In scenarios like this, it was the guy on the end of the line whom it was recommended to target first, then work your way along. Lori thought it would be more effective if she bucked the trend this once. She fired her shock blaster at the man immediately to Stockdale's left. The stun blast hit him square in the chest, knocked him to the jungle floor.

A quartet of pulse rifles ripped through the foliage. None of them came near to where Lori was, which was now a different place to where she had been.

'Close up!' yelled Stockdale. Lori thought she could afford to eliminate another of Dane's comrades before they managed to do that.

The blast slammed him against a tree.

'Grenades!' barked Stockdale.

Now things were getting serious. Lori would have to time her run precisely. Security types tended to do everything in unison, including tossing grenades. As they drew back their arms, Lori leaped to her feet. As they threw the grenades, she fled towards the plantation. They couldn't *not* see her. Their pulse rifles blazed again, but harmlessly, into a sudden concealing screen of exploding jungle.

If they were going to kill her, they'd have to come after her.

Into the plantation.

Lori was waiting for a flicker of movement from the jungle. Her eyes were blue steel, unblinking and predatory. She was on one knee, making herself a smaller target. Stockdale and his two comrades blundered into the clearing.

Stockdale and his *one* comrade opened fire on the retreating Lori.

'Stockdale!' The man called Max jabbed his finger. He'd seen the girl duck into one of the old slave huts. 'We've got her, mate.' He made to rush forward.

'Wait, you idiot!' His companion restrained him. 'This

blonde kid, if she's the girl Wolf told us about, we don't wanna be taking chances. Torch it!'

'Whooh!' Like all violent men of limited intellect, Max loved setting things on fire. He activated the pulse rifle's flame-thrower function with child-like glee.

The parched and rotting beams of the hut ignited like tinder, spouting flame into the sky. Neither man let up. The stream of fire from their weapons was constant. Cautiously, they advanced on the blazing hut.

'If she's in there, she's gotta be cooked, mate,' asserted Max almost hungrily. 'One interfering secret agent on the barbie.'

If she was in there. Out of the corner of his eye, Dane Stockdale was certain he saw a blonde and darting shape. 'Max!' He swung his pulse rifle around, an arc of flame leaping from one incinerated shelter to another yet to be touched, but which now too became an instant inferno.

'Yeah, mate! All *right*!' Max followed his companion's lead, not that he looked like he cared where he was shooting.

Stockdale, on the other hand, was planning. 'Max,' he hissed, 'if we've missed her again she'll have to fall back to the plantation house. You approach it from here. I'll go round back in case she tries for the jungle. Understand?'

'If I find her first, mate,' promised Max, 'they'll be identifying her by her dental records.'

It was a pity for Judson's men that the Covert Communications Modules at Spy High had included lip-reading techniques. From her hiding-place inside one of the barns, Lori waited for Dane Stockdale to slip away before alerting Max to her continued survival with a very poor shock blast that served only to scatter his boots with soil. She'd startled him, though. He shot wildly too as she sprinted for the stone plantation house and dived through one of the cavernous windows.

He seemed to want to end their little duel quickly now. He charged towards her with both pulse and flame-throwing options engaged. Lori crouched beneath the window and endured. The air above her was gushing with fire, singeing her hair and billowing against the far wall. The old stones were quailing before the pulse bursts. She might be roasted first or her protective wall might collapse on top of and crush her, but she couldn't move. She had to wait.

Until she could scarcely breathe and the flames almost blinded her and her skin reddened and her suit smouldered.

Until the relentless pulse bursts gashed deep wounds in the wall.

Until she had to be dead, or at least overcome by smoke and flame, helpless. Until Max had to be thinking that, was sure of it, was pausing in his brutal assault.

Lowering his weapon.

Lori snapped up. Fired once, almost without looking. If she'd judged Max's behaviour wrongly, it was game over.

She hadn't. It wasn't. The shock blast sent him sprawling in the dust.

Lori vaulted out of the window, wondering whimsically whether you could purchase an after-flame-thrower cream to soothe the skin because there'd certainly be a market for it within the espionage community. Max was lying on the ground spread-eagled and still. Even so, she approached him slowly, slowly.

To his credit, she actually *didn't* hear Dane Stockdale behind her until he cried: 'Don't move!' She froze. 'Throw your gun down and your hands up.' She obeyed. 'Now turn around and face me. Take your time.' She did that, too.

'What are you going to do with me, Mr Stockdale?' Lori asked, almost casually.

'That depends on you, blondie,' said Stockdale. 'You can either come quietly and live a little longer, or I can shoot you down right here and now. What's it to be?'

'Really, Mr Stockdale, that's hardly a choice at all, is it?' said Lori. And smiled.

THIRTEEN

Dane Stockdale was still holding Lori at gunpoint when his companions groaningly recovered from their stun blasts. Max for one seemed to resent the fact that she was alive, as if her breathing was an error in need of correction. He seemed to think he was the man for the job.

Lori, unimpressed, looked to Stockdale. 'We don't touch her,' he said. 'The Judsons' orders. I radioed to tell them we'd caught her and they want to see her, unharmed.'

'But we can mess her up a bit, mate, can't we?' Max suggested. 'Lose a few fingers here, the use of a leg there. She wouldn't look so smug with a broken jaw, now would she?' He thrust his hate-twisted face close to Lori's, as if selecting where to strike.

'We don't touch her,' repeated Stockdale flatly. 'The Judsons' *orders*.'

Max scowled. But he backed away. Obviously, even among their own men, it was deemed unwise to cross the Judsons. 'What about her weapons? Do I at least get to frisk her?'

'I've taken care of those,' said Stockdale. He was in possession of Lori's belt, blaster and wristbands. 'Now let's not keep the brothers waiting any longer. Angel, *move.*'

Lori trudged through the jungle. She made no attempt to escape her captors. The status of her mission had moved on. At least now she could be certain of getting into the Judsons' base of operations.

'So how long have you been on St Dominguez, Stockdale?' she asked. 'Since your most unfortunate death? You must like the place.'

'I like what we're doing here,' Stockdale allowed.

'What exactly *are* you doing here?'

'If they want you to know, the Judsons'll tell you themselves. Keep moving.'

'I guess you do get some holiday time, though, hey?' Lori changed tack. 'Otherwise your wife wouldn't have seen you in Sacramento. I spoke to Susan, by the way. Don't you think you owe her more than a disappearing act and a ruined reputation after we take the Judsons down, which is gonna happen – you must know that.'

'You're the one living on borrowed time, Angel, not us,' Stockdale pointed out. 'And when Susan learns the truth, she'll understand. She'll *approve*. Now shut up.'

Lori was happy to. There were suddenly other demands on her attention. The jungle fell away and the small group neared the centre of the island. Its prominent features had not been identified by the Deveraux satellites. A series of square, circular and flat-roofed concrete buildings, each some ten storeys high and linked by covered bridges, formed a ring on the exposed land. One of them boasted a heli-pad. Their windows, such as they were, made from glasteel, probably, were long, narrow slits, like suspicious eyes. Bunker mentality, Lori judged. They think the world's against them.

Then she saw what was going on outside the buildings, and she wondered if the world wasn't right to be.

Dozens of men of different races, different colours, but all in the prime of life, all physically impressive and, despite a variety of clothing from military uniform to oil-stained vests and combat trousers, all working at their one common task with fearsome discipline. They were firing weapons. *Judson* weapons, Lori had no doubt. At targets and into the air. Blasters and rifles and laser guns and handheld grenade launchers and a range of firearms that from this distance she could not recognise. A class of students highly eager to please their teachers – instructors garbed in the same fatigues as Stockdale, Max and the others. She expected the likes of Tab Allenby and Karl Kreuser to be among them. She did not expect the purpose of the training to be for the greater good.

From the roof of one of the complex's buildings, a great satellite dish pointed its aerial to the sky. At its tip, raw power crackled and coruscated – the source of the energy barrier. Lori gazed at it longingly. It couldn't be put out of action quickly enough.

'No time for sightseeing, Angel.' Stockdale shoved her with the barrel of his pulse rifle. 'The brothers want you inside.'

They were waiting for her in the building with the heli-pad, in a long room like the board-room of a company, complete with polished mahogany table and high-backed chairs. There were guards outside the door but only Dane Stockdale escorted her in. Portraits of departed Judsons and paintings of violence in which their products featured prominently decorated the walls; taking pride of place on a column at the far end of the room, perhaps unsurprisingly, was a marble bust of Irving Judson. Two of his descendents stood on either side of it. Wolf, Lori had seen too often already, though never in army fatigues. Chase Judson, on the other hand, greyer than in Jake's presentation, and dressed identically to his brother, was new to her. From his general demeanour, he was likely to be no less hostile.

'So *this* is Lori Angel?' Chase regarded her with dismissive contempt. 'You must be slipping, Wolf. She doesn't look like much to me. My brother warned me you might be paying us a visit, young lady,' he said, addressing her directly. 'Do you know who I am?'

'I've seen holograms,' Lori said. 'I've read your obituary. Such nice things they wrote. Pity none of them are true.'

'Ah, yes, my obituary,' Chase said, amused. 'I'm afraid the rumours of my death have been greatly exaggerated.'

'Doesn't look like you're the only one,' Lori observed. 'You've got yourselves a real little resurrection business going on. And here was me thinking all you Judsons were interested in was death.'

'Only for the right people, Ms Angel,' qualified Chase. Whose smile was, if anything, more lupine than his brother's.

'And am I one of those people?' Lori ventured.

'My dear girl –' the icy chuckle ran in the family, too – 'I'm sure you'd be disappointed if I pretended otherwise.'

'And is the president?'

Chase Judson chose to answer a different, as yet

unposed question. 'It was necessary for us to seem to perish in order to devote ourselves entirely to our work – to prepare for the great day that is coming and the new age that will follow it.'

'Care to tell me what any of that actually means?' Lori goaded.

Chase merely smiled and turned to his brother. 'I take it back, Wolf,' he apologised. 'You were right. She does have a certain spark. I'm sure Diana would have liked her.'

'Is Diana around here, too?' The whereabouts of the third and youngest Judson sibling began to seem important to Lori, she wasn't quite sure why. *Intuition.* A mental tool for a secret agent like any other. 'Your big family argument, Diana disappearing, none of that was for real, was it?'

'Our sister is elsewhere, Lori.' Wolf spoke for the first time. 'You will not be making her acquaintance.'

'If she's anything like the two of you,' Lori snorted, 'I'm grateful.'

'Why, you little —' It seemed that Dane Stockdale was about to prove his loyalty and affection for the Judson family by striking Lori down with a blow from the butt of his pulse rifle.

Chase stayed him with a glare. 'That will not be necessary, Stockdale. In fact, you may go. We're sure you must have duties to attend to. Ms Angel is quite safe here with us.'

'Sir.' Dane Stockdale obeyed. Lori watched him march briskly from the room. She bit her lower lip anxiously. Time was pressing.

'Tell me, Lori,' said Wolf, 'what happened to that

charmless boyfriend of yours? I thought you might have done so much better for yourself. Did he die of his wounds?'

'Cas is fine,' reported Lori.

'I'm sorry to hear it. If I have a chance after the event, perhaps I'll rectify the matter.'

'*What* event? What are you talking about?'

'Come, come, my dear girl,' encouraged Chase, easing into a chair. 'You're supposed to be the secret agent, aren't you? Prove it. You tell us.'

'All right,' said Lori. She thought she had a good idea. 'What you've done so far is turn St Dominguez into one huge terrorist training camp. Madmen and malcontents from all over the world are gathered here and supplied with Judson-made arms, no doubt earning you a healthy profit. What you're *going* to do is assassinate President Westwood because he stands for everything you hate – government, compromise, order, law.'

'Not bad,' conceded Chase, 'but all you have seen, Ms Angel, is a shadow of our true intent. The reality is rather more ambitious. Your imagination, I am afraid, has been limited by convention. Your thinking has been restricted because you foolishly follow the rules. Perhaps you even *believe* in them, in outdated notions of good and evil. No. Let me tell you. St Dominguez has become more than a terrorist training camp, as you put it. Our friends among those who technically own this island have given us carte blanche to do with it what we will, and my brother and I have chosen to make a new nation of it, an *assassin* nation. Yes, our first target is to be the woeful president of the decadent United States – and I imagine if we stopped there many would actually cheer us. But we do not intend to stop there, Ms Angel. The death of one man, however powerful or influential, can never be sufficient for a Judson. The death of Westwood is to be the spark, the spark that will ignite a raging fire of revolutions. Across the world, in every major industrialised country, at the announcement of the president's assassination the soldiers we have trained here will rise up and with our weapons strike a coordinated and deadly blow at the heart of their societies. A fatal blow. Governments will topple. The rule of law will collapse. The cosy, comfortable world in which you have lived will be no more. Democracy? A creed for the weak, a betrayal of the strong, an excuse for the cringing, cowering many to dictate to the bold and unfearing few. Democracy will end. There will be no more restraint on those of us with the wit and the will to take what we want. A new age *will* dawn, Ms Angel, not an age of anarchy, but the era of *gunarchy*, and those who wield the weapons will rule the world.'

'Is that right?' Lori scoffed. 'I'll remember that when you're serving thirty to life in a penal satellite.'

Chase Judson indulged himself with a chuckle. Wolf made it stereo. 'But there's more to come. Our new age, Ms Angel, consider yourself blessed.'

'What do you mean?'

'Yours is the privilege of becoming its first victim.'

Lori was removed before the Judsons activated Irving's eyes. The bust of the founder of the family's fortune was not there, it seemed, solely for display. Its eyes projected a holographic image of a woman. The image was live. The woman the brothers knew.

'Diana,' said Chase, 'we have the brat in our custody. Soon she will no longer be even a *potential* threat to our plans.'

'I'm pleased to hear it,' said the woman. 'What with Wolf letting her escape twice, and losing the canyon house into the bargain, I was beginning to think I might have to break cover and bail you two boys out.'

'Minor setbacks, Diana, nothing more,' Wolf bridled. 'Perhaps if your report on Lori Angel had been less dismissive, *I* might have been better prepared.'

'She was blonde,' Diana Judson justified herself. 'She looked like a bimbo.'

'Appearances, dear sister, can be deceptive,' observed Chase. 'Take your own, for example. But let us not quarrel. Wolf and I are both grateful for the intelligence with which your position has enabled you to supply us. It seems sensible, however, to move our plans forward a little. Angel is soon to join her namesakes, but doubtless there will be other agents. St Dominguez is no longer safe for us. We will therefore be despatching our team forthwith.'

'You know what to do, Diana,' said Wolf.

'Of course I know what to do, Wolf,' snorted his sister indignantly.

'Keep Westwood at Lincoln. When you receive our final signal, eliminate the electronic defences.'

'Wolf,' said Diana Judson, 'if I don't receive your final signal soon, I shan't wait for the team. I'll go to Plan B and eliminate more than the defence systems. I'll assassinate the president myself.'

They led her into a small covered arena and left her

there. Okay, Lori thought. It wasn't as good as freedom but it was better than a cell. She'd been in so many of those since she joined Spy High that she could have made major contributions to 'The Good Cell Guide 2066'. The arena was bowl-shaped, about fifty metres across, with four exits, all locked. Part of the wall was glasteel, providing a view of one of the covered bridges that connected the various buildings in the complex. The visible bridge was linked to the building crowned by the satellite dish, which Lori assumed also contained the facility's control centre. That was potentially good, though at the moment fell into the 'so near yet so far' category. She returned her attention to the arena. It was rimmed by a viewing gallery, too high above the floor for her to access without clingskin. And cameras. There were more cameras hanging from the ceiling. Whatever had taken place in the arena, or was *going* to take place, somebody liked it *filmed*. Lori somehow doubted that whatever it was would be appropriate for family entertainment.

Maybe she'd find out. Chase and Wolf Judson appeared in the viewing gallery. They wore matching smiles of smugness.

'The beard and ponytail look, Wolf,' Lori hailed, 'which, by the way, is *so* twentieth-century – is that just so the rest of us can tell you and your brother apart? Don't you think little badges with your names on would have been better?'

'Thank you for the advice, Lori,' said Wolf. 'I have some for you in return. Say your prayers. Now.'

The four doors hissed open. A figure appeared in each of them. Three men, one woman. They all wore combat jackets and trousers, though the men's jackets were sleeveless. They all wore boots, except for the woman, whose feet and lower legs were shod in what appeared oddly to be some kind of reinforced surgical stocking – in black. None of them seemed to be bearing weapons.

Lori backed into the centre of the arena. 'Who are these guys? Not more relatives, I hope.'

'We thought you might like to meet the team who are about to depart for Camp Lincoln to kill the President of the United States,' said Wolf. 'Feel free to wish them well.'

'I don't think so.' If the Judsons knew about Camp Lincoln, that meant Westwood was in dire danger. On the other hand, Lori thought grimly, so was she.

Time. If it didn't happen soon, hers could be running out . . .

'We thought the team might like to undergo one final test of their new weaponry before they leave for their moment of destiny,' added Chase. 'A baptism of blood, so to speak. *Your* blood, Ms Angel. Begin.'

Gungrafts. Lori was expecting them before they revealed themselves. It didn't make her feel any better. She assumed a defensive posture, breathed deeply. As the skin peeled back from the first man's fist like the flesh of a fruit, and beneath it his forearm flattened, rounded, and then sharpened and whirred and was the razor-glinting teeth of a buzz-saw. Lori controlled her breathing, kept it slow, deep, calm. Panic would be her undoing. She would not panic. As the second man's metal arm hollowed, like a steel snake, and a lash of cable flickered from its mouth like a tongue. As the third's hands became twin electrodes, shimmering with current.

Lori emptied her mind of everything but her combat training. There was no past for her, no future: only now. As the woman's heels broadened for balance and her feet thinned, bladed, gleamed.

The Judsons' team advanced upon her. The doors closed behind them. No exit there.

It was at times like these that Lori wished she still worked with partners.

She drew up her fists to protect her face, raised one leg waist-high, balanced on the sole of her other foot. Let her enemies come to her. Four to one. Her every movement had to count.

Electrodes was the most eager. He lunged forward, his arms like pincers snapping at her head. There was a space between them. Lori kicked, a single fluid, practised motion. Her boot cracked under his chin and floored him.

Then she was ducking low as Buzz-Saw sliced the air above her, and jabbing at his solar plexus. A blow to his back followed as he doubled up in pain.

Surging up, Lori leaped high to avoid the dagger-thrust of the woman's foot, then connected in descent with the rear of her knee to send her attacker crumpling to the floor.

The lash shot out from her remaining foe's arm. Lori arched back as far as possible without snapping her spine, let the lash fish for air. Grabbed it. Ignored the pain of the voltage it carried. Yanked the cable hard. Pulled the man into contact with her fist.

She took a quick breath as her opponents gathered themselves to attack again. Tried to shut out the cameras, the watching Judsons.

'Try to stay alive a little longer if you can, Lori,' laughed Wolf. 'If this doesn't interest buyers in our weapons-grafting technology, nothing will.'

Buzz-Saw thrust at her again. From behind this time, to her right. At least the whirring of his blade gave her decent notice of his whereabouts. Lori swayed to the left. The teeth bit at the shoulder of her jacket, shaving material but not skin. With lightning speed she seized Buzz-Saw's jacket, heaved him, threw him. 'If you're cutting edge,' she grunted, 'here's where you go blunt.' His saw-hand carved into the floor, stuck there. One further blow now while he was helpless and four would become three.

But no. The woman's dagger-feet were stabbing at her again. Lori needed all her agility to avoid them.

And then Electrodes struck again too. Just scraping her side with one of them caused Lori's body to lance with agony. She fired off a reflex combination of blows that staggered him. But she was slower. The pain was slowing her down.

She had to fight it.

Blade-Feet gashed her calf. Now there was blood, a thin spray. Lori sent her reeling with a well-placed elbow just as the cable wrapped around her neck. It tightened, a garotte. Lori choked.

Electrodes pressed forward and Buzz-Saw had freed himself, was returned to the fray.

Lori twisted like a fish on a line. Buzz-Saw's arc slit open her jacket at the side. She'd suffered worse cuts before. Electrodes's blow she fended off with her arm. The paralysis would wear off. She hoped. But she had to free herself from the cable fast.

Lori propelled herself backwards, directly into her assailant. Hit him hard, hauled him over her back, used him as a missile against his comrades.

But they didn't all fall. Electrodes ran at her again and there was no way to avoid him.

She should have listened to Cas.

Electrodes piled into her.

Lori felt that her nervous system was on fire and that flames were scorching through her limbs and that her mind and soul were shrivelling in the blaze.

She was on the floor. She was on her knees.

She hadn't listened. She'd rolled the dice again. She'd gambled and she'd lost.

Fight it! part of her screamed. *Fight the pain!* But she couldn't. It was too great. It was too much.

The Judsons were standing far above her like Caesars from the age of the gladiators and they had only to give the word.

She was dead.

FOURTEEN

Two things happened. It seemed to Lori, as the pain crashed against her in waves like the surf against the rocks, that they happened simultaneously, and there was a quality of unreality about them both.

She heard a new voice, a warning voice. Through blurred vision she thought she saw a man in combat fatigues jabbering to the Judsons. Her four assailants thought they were seeing it too: their attention was distracted.

And the glasteel window was erupting inwards as if commencing a new career as a volcano. Half of the wall exploding with it. The building shook. Flame and stone spouted across the arena.

Lori was on the floor, the debris spraying over her head. Her tormentors were standing. But not for long.

And from the vent in the wall, a mouth of sudden shock, came the clatter of guns and the drone of rotor blades and the booming crescendos of falling bombs. The complex was under attack.

Lori fought for her consciousness as she clung to that

one irrefutable fact. *The complex was under attack*. The energy barrier was down. The Deveraux chip had worked.

One realisation led to another. She wasn't dead.

And she wasn't going to be.

So she was hurting. That wasn't new. And if her pain was like the surf against the rocks, then the oceans ebbed and flowed and in the end were calm. The rocks endured. They survived. As Lori would survive.

Her limbs screamed for mercy but she forced them to do their work. She stood. Around her, three of the members of the terrorist team scheduled to murder the president lay unconscious. Buzz-Saw sat sobbing as he cradled his cutting arm: the blade was shattered and useless.

'Looks . . . it looks,' Lori struggled, 'like the assass . . . ination . . . might have to be postponed . . . boys.'

'You did this!' Wolf snarled with rage. 'Somehow, you did it, Angel!' His left fist punched its way out of its skin like a paper bag. His own gungraft relished its liberty. 'I should have dealt with you myself in the first place.'

Lori was already running, though every pounding stride shot agony through her body. 'Easy . . . to say that now, Wolf.' His bullets tore after her. She could have been back in Judson's house in the Grand Canyon. 'But then . . . life is a learning experience. And have I got a lesson for you!' The arena seethed with ammunition at her feet. She launched herself through the gaping hole in the wall.

It was like leaping into the final reel of an action movie. Government helicopters swarmed in the sky like angry wasps, missiles firing and machine guns rattling, raking the complex. Several of the round buildings were already on fire. The defence systems of all were retaliating. Where human voices could be heard above the mechanical sounds of carnage, they were shouting, screaming, desperate. All this Lori absorbed in a single chaotic second.

Across from her was the covered bridge.

It had already been hit and the side nearest to her had collapsed inwards. Helpful. Now she could gain access to the interior of the complex and make a faster way to the control centre. She hadn't forgotten the Judson brothers but they would have to wait. She had a more pressing engagement with Dane Stockdale first.

Lori leaped inside the bridge as lithely as she could manage while bleeding in several places. Among the rubble were several unconscious bodies. Those of the Judsons' men who still had their wits about them charged frantically past her in one direction or the other as if she was wearing a fully functioning chameleon suit. It was always the way during battle: participants tended to lose sight of everything but their own survival, particularly the bad guys' lackeys who were usually only in it for the money and lacked the stomach to perish for a cause. Lori wasn't complaining. It meant that no one tried to stop her as she raced into the building with the satellite dish.

She needed to get there quickly before the whole thing went up in flames. A man in a white coat and with a face to match attempted to flee past her. 'Wait!' Lori swung him round and slammed him against the wall.

'Let go of me! Let me go!' Like a tearful child accosted by a policeman.

'Where's the control centre?' A low moan escaped the man's throat but nothing more useful. 'Don't make me ask you again!' threatened Lori.

'Next floor up. Next floor up! Please . . .'

Lori let him go. Maybe next time he'd settle for a job with IBM.

Stockdale, she thought. I'm on my way.

The white coated man's information was correct. A flight of stairs, cracking in the middle as the building's battering continued, led Lori to a large room which, even before most of its occupants had scattered, would have contained more computers than people. Much of the roof had fallen in. Blocks of concrete had crushed keyboards and shattered screens. Cables and wires bulged exposed from the ceiling like intestines. Small fires had broken out in every part of the control centre. Apart from Lori, the only personnel present were either injured and groaning, unconscious, or worse.

'Stockdale!' she cried out, not immediately seeing him. 'Stockdale!'

For Dane Stockdale, it was worse.

Evidence of combat led her to him, the bodies, not of comtechs, but of soldiers with automatic weapons, *Judson* weapons. Soldiers who seemed to have been mown down by someone from within the room, not by the attacking special services. Lori knew who. He was lying beneath a scrum of his former comrades who'd finally overpowered and put an end to him.

The Deveraux chip had worked only too well on Dane Stockdale.

Back among the plantation buildings Angel Blue had deliberately left Stockdale to last. It had been part of the plan. Because however fleetly the older man felt he could move, Angel Blue had been trained to be quicker. Because after 'incapacitating the host', as Ferns would no doubt have phrased it, she'd taken the cranial syringe from its pouch in her belt and injected the chip into Stockdale's brain. Because from then on, from the moment he recovered consciousness and believed that he'd been holding her captive the whole time, Dane Stockdale had been little more than a human animate, like the construct Lori had encountered in his coffin – at the mercy of another's program.

It had been Stockdale who'd gone, not about his duties but to the control centre. Stockdale who'd disabled the energy barrier and ushered the government forces in, one of the last men who would be suspected of betrayal short of the Judson brothers themselves.

He'd paid a heavy price for his unwitting alliance with the Deveraux organisation. The next time a funeral was held for Dane Stockdale, he truly would be there.

Lori knelt beside the body. She wasn't certain what she should be feeling. Relief that the Deveraux chip had worked in the field and had probably put an end to the Judsons' wild schemes and saved her life? Something stronger than relief? Joy or delight, perhaps, that the good guys were on the brink of chalking up another victory in the endless war against the armies of evil? Or, possibly, something less triumphalist, something darker, more critical, tinged with doubt and uncertainty? Because was it right to deliberately lead one man to his inevitable self-destruction in order to further a mission – to take him over, make him a robot? Did the ends justify the means?

What should she be feeling?

She tried to ignore the question by frisking the corpse of Dane Stockdale, not a pleasant duty in itself. But again, necessary. Also in the Deveraux chip program was the instruction that having disabled the energy barrier, the host should remain in the control centre under any circumstances – death was a bonus in that regard, Lori thought bitterly – until Angel Blue could make her way to him. And that he should have retained about his person her belt and wristbands.

The host had done that, too. Lori located the required objects zipped inside jacket pockets. They weren't even splattered with the host's blood. The *host*, Lori pondered. *Stockdale*. It hadn't *had* to be him. Chance had made him one of the team sent to investigate a possible intruder on St Dominguez. Lori had *chosen* him. She'd recognised him and she'd chosen him. Bottom line: Dane's death was down to her. Lori thought of Susan Stockdale, mourning her husband with his photograph on the side-board, suddenly and insanely believing him still to be alive. Not any more he wasn't.

What should she be feeling?

Lori drew on her belt, clamped on her wristbands.

It didn't matter what Lori felt, not now, not yet. On active duty an agent couldn't afford the distraction of emotion. In the field, she wasn't even Lori Angel. She was Angel Blue. And she had business to conclude with the Judson brothers.

In the long room hung with paintings, there was brisk activity. The eyes of deceased Judsons rendered in oils deigned not to take notice of the doings of their male descendents, perhaps because they seemed to involve a retreat that nobler members of the family would never have contemplated.

'We have to tell Diana,' Wolf was demanding. 'You heard her before. She can kill the president herself while we regroup.'

Chase seemed to be listening more to the commotion of gunfire and groans issuing from beyond the locked doors than to his brother. 'No time, Wolf,' he decided. 'We have to go while the heli-pad is still operational.'

He pressed down on the bust of Irving Judson. With a click, a hitherto concealed door opened slyly, revealing steps to the roof: private access to the heli-pad and a waiting chopper.

'Damn that Angel girl.' Wolf's teeth were fangs and his eyes crystals of hate. 'This is *her* fault. If I see her again I'll tear her limb from limb.'

'Forget her!' snapped Chase. 'Let's go.'

Neither directive was immediately possible. At that moment the doors, though remaining locked, nonetheless gave way. A guard crashed through and was followed by another, hurled head-first.

Lori Angel stepped over them. 'Thought I might find you here, guys, but what's this? A tactical realignment of available resources? Some would say it's just plain old running away.'

'Judsons don't run from the likes of you, girl!' Wolf snarled.

'Wolf!' his brother warned.

But nothing was going to divert him now. He raised his left arm, activating his gungraft again.

This time Lori was ready. 'Don't you ever get tired of

the same old routine?' This time she had a little surprise for Wolf, one reason why it had been vital to retrieve her belt of gadgets from Dane Stockdale. She held the device in her palm.

'Prepare to die, Angel.'

'Not today, Mr Wolf,' said Lori. Before he could shoot, she pressed the button. She energised the jammer.

Wolf's gungraft shorted out, exploded on his arm. With a cry of mingled rage and pain, he pitched forward, smashing the now useless hunk of metal on the table, splintering the perfectly polished surface. His precious firearm, the future of weapons technology, mangled and twisted. Rather like Wolf's mind, Lori reflected.

'Jamming device,' she said. 'Is that one down, one to go?'

'I'll not leave my brother.' Chase, who had been halfway through the door to the heli-pad, now thought better of it. 'Judsons stand or fall together!' He drew a shock blaster and unleashed its ammunition at Lori.

'So that's fall, then.' She dived behind a chair, retaliated with sleepshot. 'And no fancy gungrafts for you, Chase? Isn't that letting the family down?'

'I prefer to trust to more traditional killing methods.' And he was good. His shock blasts were coming close.

'Don't tell me,' Lori taunted. 'They're more efficient. Well, try this.'

She thought she had him. She thought she couldn't miss. But Chase's speed belied his years. The sleepshot shell did not strike flesh but metal, Judson's shock blaster, knocking it from his grip.

Not that Chase seemed to care. Now he was rampaging

down the side of the room towards Lori like a maddened
bull elephant. In combat fatigues.

She ought to have simply put him out of his misery
with sleepshot. But that would have been too . . . efficient. After gungrafts and animates and Deveraux chips,
Lori felt the need for that *human* touch.

She didn't back off. She didn't even simply stand her
ground. She charged to meet him.

His shouts of fury bellowing. His brawny hands
grasping. At the last moment Lori feinted, swept low
with her leg, converted Chase's momentum from his
advantage to her own. The older man cannoned into the
chairs, breaking their backs, breaking his fall. Lori
closed in to finish it. Chase's boot drove into her
stomach. *Stupid!* She cursed herself – a conscious enemy
was an enemy who could still fight.

And he was on his feet again, mounting an intelligent
attack. Chase's karate was ambitious and aggressive.
Lori blocked his blows but found it difficult to do anything but defend herself. She was being beaten
backwards, beaten down. Her body seemed already one
stinging source of pain. There'd been nothing but battle
since she'd arrived on St Dominguez. She was getting
weaker. She'd planned how to deal with Wolf, not
Chase. Should have used sleepshot, after all. No chance
at such close quarters now.

Suddenly, she was bumping up against something
hard and unyielding. The column which bore the bust of
Irving Judson.

'You're a fool, girl.' Chase's eyes burned. 'You can
defeat one Judson, perhaps, but never all of us. We are
united.'

'Yeah?' Lori saw the blow coming. She sidestepped smartly. Chase brought his hand down on his ancestor's marble head. Hard. The hand came off worst. 'You think so?' She seized the bust from its pedestal as Chase Judson shrieked. 'Tell it to Irving!' And swung it like a bat.

Chase sank senseless to the floor on the spot. The two brothers lay almost side by side. They looked so peaceful it was almost touching. Almost.

'I never thought I'd say this, Irving Judson,' Lori addressed the bust, 'but I think I love you.'

St Dominguez was preparing to be abandoned again. A handful of government techs might remain behind, it was true, with a skeleton security staff, to sift through the Judsons' computer and other resources to see if there wasn't anything that could be borrowed and put to better use by the forces of justice. But the island's most recent occupants, the terrorists and world-conquering wannabes, they were being readied for departure.

Lori looked on while a medtech dabbed at her wounds with a skin-salver like an artist adding the final thoughtful touches to a masterpiece. Those of the Judsons' men who could walk were marched in grim and sullen lines to the prisoncopters. Lori noticed that Max was among them, evidently unhappy that he'd been forced to part from his pulse rifle. Terrorists incapable after the battle of independent movement were not spared. They were carried into custody either on stretchers or in body bags. In the background the buildings of the complex were almost all on fire.

Yet Chase and Wolf Judson looked pretty chipper for

a pair of bad guys whose grand schemes had likewise gone up in flames. They were conversing quietly to each other inside a circle of guards with guns trained on them. Not that there seemed to be any chance of their making a wrong move – Chase was securely bound and Wolf's crippled gungraft arm was in a sling. Even more reason why the brothers' calm composure worried Lori.

'What's that?' A Deveraux tech was asking her a question. He repeated it. Lori winced. 'Yes, very successful. You can tell Mr Deveraux that the chip worked perfectly.' The tech said something else. 'No, the host won't be able to report for it to be removed. I doubt at this point he cares very much one way or the other.' One of the body bags held Dane Stockdale, like a strange kind of shopping. The tech was about to pursue the matter but Lori waved him away. 'Sorry, but can we do this later? I need to speak to Chase and Wolf.'

They seemed not displeased to see her. 'Well, young lady,' greeted the older brother, 'enjoy your success while you can. It will not last.'

'I'll get a new gungraft fitted, Angel,' promised Wolf, 'a better one. A firearm your wretched jamming device will not be able to affect. Then we'll meet again. Then we'll see.'

'Dream on, guys,' dismissed Lori. 'The last I heard, Wolf, they don't do gungrafts on penal satellites and that's where both of you are going to be spending the next thirty years or so. I'm afraid it's all over for the Judsons.'

'No, girl,' Chase said. 'I told you before. You can defeat one Judson, perhaps – temporarily – even two of us, but you can never defeat us all.'

'Diana.' Lori understood. 'You're talking about your sister, right?'

'If *she* underestimated *you*, Lori Angel,' said Chase, 'then you are also guilty of underestimating *her*. When Diana learns what has happened here, she will act. The president still will die. Our time will still come – an age of fire and blood and guns. It is inevitable.'

But Lori had already stopped listening to Chase Judson's rant. She'd heard it all before. 'If *she* underestimated *me*? You mean Diana's already met me? When? How is one woman going to be able to reach the president?'

Then Lori realised. Her heart chilled. It could be done if the assassin was the one woman the president trusted.

And the Judson brothers were laughing.

FIFTEEN

For a location that didn't officially exist, the presidential retreat of Camp Lincoln did not take any chances with intruders. The latest electronic defence systems could spot an insect heading the compound's way at a distance of three miles, and atomise it if it was thought to be a bug in the pay of America's enemies. There were enough soldiers, FBI men and members of a variety of other covert security agencies stationed on the premises to overrun a small country if one became available for the purpose. The most powerful man in the world was also just about the best protected.

But it was only news from an otherwise inconsequential scrap of land in the Pacific that made Graveney Westwood feel safe.

'Did you hear that? Did you *hear*?' The president clapped his hands like a child on Christmas morning, danced a little jig, no longer worried if his head bobbed like a target in front of the windows, and finally threw his arms around the body of his vice-president. 'It's done, Gayle. It's finished. The conspirators have been caught.

The assassination threat is over. Ain't that a hell of a thing?'

'Indeed, Mr President, sir.' Gayle Steinwitz might have made a comment about the unpleasantness of having one's personal space invaded with impunity, or of having one's cheeks brazenly assaulted without their consent by the presidential lips – and damp, slob-bering presidential lips they were too. But now was not the time. 'It is indeed a hell of a thing as you say.' And it wasn't going to matter for much longer, in any case.

'Graveney Westwood survives again,' trumpeted the president. 'Whatever his enemies throw at him, however clever they think they are, you know that *nothing's* gonna stand in his way. But did you hear, Gayle, it wasn't just that son of a Mississippi river rat *Wolf* Judson who was plotting against me, but his big brother Chase as well. And we all thought he was *dead*. It just goes to show, don't it, Gayle, it just goes to show –' Westwood drove the fist of one hand repeatedly into the palm of the other – 'these days you can't trust *nobody*.'

'It seems not, Mr President,' said Gayle.

'Well, give the orders.' Westwood peered out at the night sky. 'In the morning we'll head back to the White House. All these trees round here are playing hell with my asthma. Get it arranged, Gayle, then you can sleep peaceful in your bed knowing the president is safe.'

'Yes, sir.'

'I'm going for a session with Debbie. The way I'm feeling now, my therapy's going to come on in leaps and bounds. We'll be in my private rooms if you need me, Gayle, y'hear?'

'Yes, Mr President.'

A. J. Butcher

228

If she needed him. Gayle Steinwitz was unaccustomed to bursting out into spontaneous fits of laughter, but it was tempting to make an exception there. If *she*, the Iceberg, needed Graveney Westwood.

She'd show him just how much she needed or didn't need him.

Because it was time. The moment had come to act. The news from St Dominguez made that inevitable. This charade had to end.

Gayle Steinwitz sat at her desk. She unlocked a drawer and opened it. For several minutes she gazed at what was within and did not move. Then she reached for it, took hold of it, and stood.

President Graveney Westwood's day was about to take a turn for the worse.

'Ah, Debbie, y'all have no idea what a *relief* this is.' The president stretched himself out and luxuriated on the sofa in the lounge area of his private rooms. 'I'm sure as hell I'm gonna have peachy dreams tonight.'

Debbie Hunter's snub nose wrinkled. 'Does that mean you don't want to discuss *last* night's dreams, Mr President?' She was perched on a chair with a clipboard and a pen.

'No, no,' said Westwood. 'We may as well keep the program rolling. You know something, though, Debbie, Ms Hunter, *Debs*.' The president felt playful. 'You could be a real purty girl if you kind of growed your hair and applied a little bit of make-up here and there. You've never worn make-up since the day I took you on. Any reason why?'

'Make-up is a kind of deception, Mr President,' said

Debbie Hunter. 'I believe people should be who they claim to be. Now, the session? Your dreams?'

'Surely, Debbie,' said Westwood and chuckled. 'Funny thing is, though, you were *in* my dreams last night.'

'I thought our understanding was that we were never going to discuss *that* type of dream, Mr President,' said Debbie.

'No, no. It's peachy. Let me tell you what happened. I was in the senate about to give an address and I was surrounded by all these people clapping and cheering. Only they weren't all politicians, not all of 'em. Some were folks I knew outside of politics. Some were folks I'd known a long time ago, when I was still a boy in Louisiana. But they were all applauding me and calling on me to speak. So I looked down for my notes but they weren't there. Somehow, they'd vanished. And when I looked up again the people weren't cheering any more or saying anything or clapping, but they were kind of just standing there looking at me and their faces were like *accusing* me of something. And I noticed folks I hadn't noticed before. There was Wolf Judson and Chase Judson and there was Gayle there, too, and they were all kind of staring and accusing and none of them looked happy.' The memory of the dream seemed to be deflating Westwood's mood. He was sitting forward on the sofa now and his brow was furrowing. 'And then, as sudden as a summer storm, we're not in the senate any more but in some kind of Roman building with those marble pillar things that reach up to support the roof only they stretched up so high you couldn't even see the roof. And somehow we were all of us wearing togas now and everyone but me had knives – daggers. And they all hated me, I could tell. And they were closing in.'

'What did you do, Mr President?' asked Debbie Hunter with mild interest.

'Well, hell,' said Westwood, 'I did what anyone'd do, dream or no dream. I tried to get the heck out of there. I ran. I tried to get between the pillars to safety, but every time I did there was someone blocking my way, Wolf, Chase, even Gayle, all of 'em brandishing their knives. Then at last, Debbie, at last I saw *you*, and you were calling my name and beckoning me to come on over. So I did. And then, and then . . .'

'And *then*, Mr President?'

'Then there was a dagger in *your* hand, too, and your face was kind of peeling off to show something dark and terrible underneath it, and I was screaming out something that sounded like 'Eat two, Brute,' and I don't know what the heck that means . . .'

'How fascinating, Mr President,' mused Debbie Hunter. 'Perhaps there *is* something in dream analysis, after all.' She put her clipboard down, but not her pen, and stood.

'What d'you mean, Debbie?' frowned Graveney Westwood. 'You not making any more notes?'

'With this?' The therapist regarded her pen critically. 'Hardly. This thing doesn't write. It's wearing make-up, you might say.' She crossed the room to the main door.

'I don't understand,' Westwood said nervously. 'Debbie, why have you locked the door?'

'So we won't be disturbed, Mr President,' said Debbie Hunter like frost on a tombstone. 'You, me, and my pen that's *not* a pen.'

It was in fact a knife. Very long. Very thin. And very sharp.

'Debbie . . .' Westwood wobbled fearfully to his feet, too. 'What are you doing?'

'What do you *think* I'm doing, you idiot?' Debbie demanded, her face suddenly contorted with hatred and contempt. 'I'm preparing to *kill* you. God only knows how I've managed to restrain myself all this time, but I guess all good things come to those who wait.' She advanced purposefully towards Westwood, like a butcher keen to carve a carcass.

'Kill me?' the president whimpered. 'But why?'

'If I told you *that*, Westwood,' Debbie snorted, 'we'd still be here in the morning, and in matters of assassination, time is usually of the essence.'

'It's my dream! It's my dream!' squealed the most powerful man in the world. 'Nobody loves me!'

And he made a frantic dash for his bedroom door.

Not quick enough. Debbie Hunter was there first, blocking the way.

'Help me! Help!' howled the president.

'But you saw me lock the door, President Imbecile,' Debbie chuckled coldly. 'Ain't no one gonna save you now.'

'Don't bet on it, lady.' Because before the knife-wielder could move, the bedroom door was slamming open and Lori's kick was sending her sprawling.

'Who?' Westwood quivered. 'What . . . wait! I know you. You're that agent kid. What are you doing in my bedroom?'

'Waiting for your true enemy to reveal herself, Mr President,' said Lori, 'which I think she's just done. We had your lounge bugged. I heard everything.'

'Then you know it's Debbie Hunter, my therapist. She tried to kill me.'

'Not *tried*, you abject idiot,' snorted the woman in question, rising again with her blade intact. 'Try*ing*.'

'And not Debbie Hunter, therapist, either,' said Lori. 'May I introduce Diana Judson, youngest of the Judson family and soon to join her brothers in a cell.'

'Diana . . . Judson . . . ?' Westwood couldn't believe it.

'How did you realise, Angel?' said Diana.

'I knew you had to be someone close to the president,' said Lori. 'And no matter how much physical recon-struction you've undergone to become Debbie Hunter, DNA doesn't lie. We took a sample of your brothers' and checked it against the DNA records that have to be kept on all members of the White House staff. It was a match. Besides, Debbie *Hunter*? Come on, anyone with a half-decent education knows that Diana was the Roman goddess of hunting.' Lori squared up to Diana Judson, prepared to do a little hunting of her own. 'We only released news of your brothers' capture after I'd got here. You fell right into our trap or – in other words, want to surrender yet?'

'What do you think?' growled Diana. 'I'll do to you just what I did to that interfering boy back in LA. He was one of your organisation, wasn't he?'

Simon? It had been Diana Judson who'd stabbed Simon? 'You shouldn't have said that, Diana,' said Lori. 'He was a friend of mine.'

'Good,' spat Diana. 'Then you won't mind joining him, will you?'

She lunged with her knife. Lori sidestepped neatly, paralysed her attacker's forearm with a karate blow. The blade fell to the carpet. Make it quick, she thought, before the anger at the back of her mind grew and she was tempted to do Diana Judson some real damage, some *Jake* damage. But the woman wasn't beaten yet. She lashed at Lori with her other arm, was blocked. Lori let Diana press the initiative, drew her forward.

Then with viper swiftness she was seizing the older woman's shoulders, falling backwards and pulling Diana down with her, sinking her foot into the Judson's stomach and propelling her head-over heels through the air.

She crashed heavily on to her back but Diana Judson might still just have managed to get up again and continue the fight. Had President Graveney Westwood not by then fumbled the door unlocked to allow the entry of several marines with rifles, rifles that they pointed squarely at her like accusing fingers.

'That was for Simon,' Lori said, grateful in a way that the marines were here to discourage her from further violence. 'Had enough?'

'Judsons never surrender,' defied Diana. 'They simply bide their time. One day, Lori Angel, we will meet again.'

'Funny, that,' said Lori. 'Wolf said the same thing. Guess vague and vacuous threats run in the family.' Two of the soldiers hauled Diana Judson to her feet. 'But hey, Diana? This meeting again stuff? Not if I see you first.'

They'd taken Diana Judson away. The marines had left, too. Lori was about to follow them when the president grabbed her by the hand.

'Don't go. Please,' Graveney Westwood pleaded.

'Don't leave me.' His eyes were big with fear and his shoulders cringed. He was shaking like a child terrified of monsters under the bed.

This was the President. If the voters could only see him now, Lori mused.

'It's okay. It's all right now, Mr President,' she soothed. 'Diana's gone.'

'No. You don't understand,' Westwood insisted. 'My dream. They *all* hate me. You don't realise. Everybody's after me. You are the only one I can trust.'

'Surely that's not true, Mr President.' Lori patted his hands reassuringly, taking advantage of the gesture to unclasp them from her own. She wanted to add 'there, there' but at the last moment changed her mind to 'Look, here's Vice-President Steinwitz. You can trust her, can't you?'

'Gayle?' Westwood didn't seem immediately convinced.

Gayle Steinwitz entered the room. 'I heard about the attack,' she said coolly. 'So Debbie Hunter was Diana Judson, hmm? It's a day of surprises, isn't it? I was coming to see you anyway, Mr President.'

'What's that in your hand, Gayle?' said Westwood nervously.

The vice-president lifted the piece of paper to her eyes as if to check. 'It's my letter of resignation, Mr President,' she said. 'I didn't want to submit it while there was still a clear and present danger to your life – it might have damaged my future prospects – but now the Judson threat has been removed, well . . . Mr President, I resign.'

'You *what*?' gaped Westwood. 'You *resign*? Gayle, you can't! You can't do this to me!'

'I think you'll find I can, Mr President,' said Gayle Steinwitz. 'And I think you'll find I have. I don't want to be a part of this incompetent apology of an administration for a moment longer. Goodbye, Mr President. I'd like to be able to say it's been a pleasure working with you, but I can't. Now if you'll excuse me, I have bags to pack.'

Gayle permitted her letter of resignation to flutter to the floor, turned smartly on her heel, and left. She closed the door firmly behind her.

'Gayle! Gayle? You can't leave me!' bleated President Graveney Westwood. 'What am I gonna do without you?' He scrabbled on the floor for the letter. 'What am I gonna do? What . . .?' He suddenly seemed to remember Lori's presence. He looked up at her, flashed the Westwood vote-winning smile – big and manly and entirely artificial. 'Hey, Angel, you wanna be vice-president?'

Lori managed to resist the allure of political office, much in the same way a person might conquer the temptation to go swimming in crocodile-infested waters. She thanked Graveney Westwood – it was always a good idea to be polite to presidents – but then she left Camp Lincoln. There was somewhere else she needed to be.

On the fourth day after Robbie Royal's admission to hospital in Las Vegas, Lori was back to see him.

She walked down the shiny hospital corridors excitedly, trying not to run. Her narrow escapes from death on St Dominguez, the revived memory of what had happened to poor Simon Macey, her entire Spy High lifestyle, they weren't reasons to drive her and Casino apart. In fact, the exact opposite was true, they were reasons to bring the two of them together. Because life was about taking chances, life was about risks. For everyone. There was risk in taking your wheelless out for a spin. There was risk in crossing a road. But if you *didn't* cross the occasional road, you'd never get anywhere. The best way forward, the *only* way, Lori thought, was to accept risk as inevitable and to compensate for it by living each and every day to the full. Take your chances before they pass you by, perhaps for ever.

If you like a boy, tell him. And tell him *now*. Before it's too late.

That was what Lori had it in mind to do as she turned the corner into Casino's corridor. And hesitated. No guard on the door of his private room? No cause for alarm, she tried to assure herself. Now that the Judsons were in custody, there was no need to protect Cas from them. But even so . . .

It wasn't done to run in hospital corridors. Lori didn't care.

She reached Casino's room, flung the door open.

An old man was being spoon-fed soup by a nurse with the body of a wrestler.

'Can I help you?' said the nurse.

'Casino . . . Robbie Royal,' Lori stammered. 'I thought this was *his* room . . .'

'Not any more, honey,' said the nurse.

'Why . . . I mean, has he been moved? I thought he was supposed to be here until tomorrow.'

'Moved himself, honey,' supplied the nurse. 'Checked out of his own accord yesterday, more like this was a hotel than a hospital.'

'Didn't you stop him?' Lori snapped angrily, bitterly. 'Didn't anyone stop him?'

'It's a free country, honey, ain't you heard? 'Sides, we needed the bed.'

Lori bit her lip. 'Of course. I'm sorry.' What had she been thinking? *If you like a boy, tell him. Before it's too late.*

Welcome to too late.

'Boy who was here,' said the nurse, 'he mean something to you, honey?'

Lori smiled ruefully. 'He might have done,' she said.

The students had gone to shower and change. Their mothers had come to collect them. The lesson was over.

Good thing, too, brooded Lori. It meant she could get a good start on today's moping time. She'd been indulging in a lot of that since her return to the Carmody Dance Academy a week ago. Sitting around – sometimes standing, it wasn't all the same thing – and thinking about a certain somebody. A certain somebody she hadn't been able to track down in Vegas and who to locate by employing the full might of the Spy High satellite surveillance system would be, according to Jonathan Deveraux himself, an erroneous prioritisation of resources. Or, in other words, no chance.

So she was back teaching little girls to moon mood, back to waiting for the next crisis in world security. Back where she'd started.

At least Jake wasn't around to say 'I told you so'.

She heard the someone in the studio doorway before she turned to look at them. It was probably Eleanor Kiley once more, playing out the 'Chrissie's so much happier now that you're back' routine again like a rerun on videvision.

It wasn't.

'Excuse me, but I understand there's an instructor here who can teach me the lambada.'

'Cas!' Of course it was Cas, leaning nonchalantly in the doorway, brown eyes twinkling and hair kind of spiky. He was smiling. So was Lori, she felt her muscles move instinctively, even though she felt she had a right to scowl. 'Cas, you . . . where have you *been*?'

'Oh, around.' He raised a hand as Lori advanced towards him. 'You're gonna be gentle with me, right? My side's still a bit sore.'

'Gentle? I ought to throw you out of here.'

'Could be worse, I guess.'

'What did you think you were doing, leaving the hospital, running off without telling anyone where you were going?'

'It was more like limping off than running,' corrected Casino, 'and I just needed time. Time to think. It's not something I'm renowned for.'

'You surprise me.'

'I've been here in LA for a while,' Cas said. 'Found your school. Very nice. Saw Ms Carmody – from a distance. Waited for you to come back. If you did I figured that meant you'd put old Wolf in his place once and for all. If you didn't, well, I was just kind of glad when you *did*.'

'But that was a week ago, Cas,' Lori pointed out. 'How come it's taken you this long to . . .?'

'I had to make my decision, Lori,' Casino said. 'Once and for all. So the Judsons are history, yeah?'

'Like bows and arrows.'

'But there'll be another bad guy along sooner or later. Another mission.'

'Cas,' sighed Lori, 'you know there will. You know the situation. I thought we'd said all there is to say on the subject of my work. Why did you come here if . . .?'

Casino interrupted her. 'No, Lori, not *all*. I've got something to add.' He paused. 'Is that a drum-roll I can hear, or am I imagining it? Okay, this is what I want to tell you. I don't mind, Lori. I don't care. I can't change what you do and who you are and I'm not sure now why I might ever have wanted to. Who you are looks good to me. I'm rolling the dice, Lori. I'm putting all my money on blonde. That is, of course, if you're still interested?'

'If I'm still interested? Hmm.' Lori narrowed her eyes in exaggerated meditation. 'Well, actually, Cas, I've been thinking too. About how on earth any kind of relationship can work between a fine, upstanding secret agent and a small-time hustler from the streets of Vegas.'

'Yeah?' Casino worried. 'So did you reach any conclusions, Lori? How can it work?'

'Oh,' smiled Lori. 'Easily.'

She took Casino's hand and led him on to the floor. 'Studio,' she commanded. 'Rio.' And suddenly in the Carmody Academy it was carnival.

'Not the lambada,' gulped Casino Royal.

'Cas,' said Lori, 'let's *dance*.'

About the Author

A. J. Butcher has been aware of the power of words since avoiding a playground beating aged seven because he 'told good stories'. He's been trying to do the same thing ever since. Writing serial stories at school that went on forever gave him a start (if not a finish). A degree in English Literature at Reading University kept him close to books, while a subsequent career as an advertising copywriter was intended to keep him creative. As it seemed to be doing a better job of keeping him inebriated, he finally became an English teacher instead. His influences include Dickens and Orwell, though Stan Lee, creator of the great Marvel super-heroes, is also an inspirational figure. In his spare time, A. J. reads too many comics, listens to too many '70s records and rants about politics to anyone who'll listen. When he was younger and fantasising about being a published author, he always imagined he'd invent a dashing, dynamic pseudonym for himself. Now that it's happened, however, he's sadly proven too vain for that. A. J. Butcher is his real and only name.

EDWARD RED

Spy High Series 2

A. J. Butcher

Eddie Nelligan is a graduate of the Deveraux College, a highly secret school for teenage spies. He's just been assigned his first solo mission – finding the perpetrators of a devastating missile assault on the sky-bridge linking Britain to continental Europe. The only clue points to the charismatic billionaire Bartholomew Knight. Which is kind of a problem for Eddie because he's just starting dating Knight's daughter.

EDWARD RED is the explosive new all-action spy novel from the author of the brilliant Spy High series. And unless its hero stops thinking about girls and starts investigating the mysterious Pendragon Project it could also be about the end of the world.

BENJAMIN WHITE

Spy High Series 2

A. J. Butcher

Benjamin Stanton, Jr. is a graduate of the Deveraux
College, the highly secret school for teenage spies.
When Spy High's old enemy, President Vlad Tepesch
of Wallachia, steals an alien device from a Deveraux
Moon Colony, Ben's mission is pretty straightforward:
get it back. Standing between Ben and his goal are
enemy soldiers, ferocious vampires, a jealous rival, and
a singularly disturbing prophecy. Clearly this won't be
as easy as it sounds. Bond Team has already lost one
member battling the Wallachian president – could
Benjamin Stanton be next?

From the author of the fabulous EDWARD RED and
ANGEL BLUE, comes BENJAMIN WHITE: the
new all-action spy novel about duty, honour and
friendship. And evil dictators trying to use an alien
device to destroy the world.

SPY HIGH
Series One

EPISODE ONE:

The Frankenstein Factory

ISBN 1904233139   £5.00

EPISODE TWO:

The Chaos Connection

ISBN 1904233147   £5.00

EPISODE THREE:

The Serpent Scenario

ISBN 1904233155   £5.00

EPISODE FOUR:

The Paranoia Plot

ISBN 1904233163   £5.00

EPISODE FIVE:

The Soul Stealer

ISBN 1904233171   £5.00

EPISODE SIX:

The Annihilation Agenda

ISBN 190423318X   £5.00

www.spyhigh.co.uk

www.atombooks.co.uk

THE FRANKENSTEIN FACTORY

Spy High Series 1: Episode 1

A. J. Butcher

Somewhere in the not too distant future, there is a school that is much more than it seems. To the outside world it is known as The Deveraux College for talented teenagers. But to Lori, Jake and the other new first years, it goes by a very different name: Spy High.

Those who pass its rigorous training program will become the world's best hope in the fight against evil megalomaniacs and crazed techno-terrorists. Those who fail will have their memories erased.

Let the lessons begin . . .